"Find a place to sit. I'll be right with…"

You.

Kate felt a sudden disconnect between her brain and her voice when she spotted the man standing just inside the entrance, backlit by the morning sun.

Alex Porter, in the flesh.

In *her* café.

She'd sat right next to Abby in church the day before and her friend hadn't warned—*told*—her that Alex would be in Mirror Lake.

A week early.

Their eyes met over the counter and Kate's heart did a backflip. As impossible as it seemed, the man was even more good-looking than she remembered.

"Abby sounded a little stressed out the last time I talked to her," he said. The rough velvet voice had a serrated edge that immediately put Kate on the defensive. "I decided to drive up a few days early to help out."

Kate knew better. Men like Alex Porter didn't help out. They took over. And the guy probably didn't have a clue that *he'd* been the cause of Abby's stress.

Books by Kathryn Springer

Love Inspired

Tested by Fire
Her Christmas Wish
By Her Side
For Her Son's Love
A Treasure Worth Keeping
Hidden Treasures
Family Treasures
Jingle Bell Babies
*A Place to Call Home
*Love Finds a Home
*The Prodigal Comes Home
The Prodigal's Christmas Reunion
*Longing for Home

*Mirror Lake

Steeple Hill Single Title

Front Porch Princess
Hearts Evergreen
 "A Match Made for
  Christmas"
Picket Fence Promises
The Prince Charming List

KATHRYN SPRINGER

is a lifelong Wisconsin resident. Growing up in a "newspaper" family, she spent long hours as a child plunking out stories on her mother's typewriter and hasn't stopped writing since! She loves to write inspirational romance because it allows her to combine her faith in God with her love of a happy ending.

Longing for Home
Kathryn Springer

Love Inspired

Recycling programs
for this product may
not exist in your area.

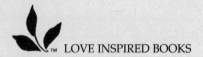 LOVE INSPIRED BOOKS

ISBN-13: 978-0-373-08218-6

LONGING FOR HOME

www.LoveInspiredBooks.com

Printed in U.S.A.

Dear Reader,

Welcome to Love Inspired!

2012 is a very special year for us. It marks the fifteenth anniversary of Love Inspired. Hard to believe that fifteen years ago, we first began publishing our warm and wonderful inspirational romances.

Back in 1997, we offered readers three books a month. Since then we've expanded quite a bit! In addition to the heartwarming contemporary romances of Love Inspired, we have the exciting romantic suspenses of Love Inspired Suspense, and the adventurous historical romances of Love Inspired Historical. Whatever your reading preference, we've got fourteen books a month for you to choose from now!

Throughout the year we'll be celebrating in several different ways. Look for books by bestselling authors who've been writing for us since the beginning, stories by brand-new authors you won't want to miss, special miniseries in all three lines, reissues of top authors and much, much more.

This is our way of thanking you for reading Love Inspired books. We know our uplifting stories of hope, faith and love touch your hearts as much as they touch ours.

Join us in celebrating fifteen amazing years of inspirational romance!

Blessings,

Melissa Endlich and Tina James
Senior Editors of Love Inspired Books

In loving memory of Lois A. Goldsmith
June 29, 1916–February 27, 2011

* * *

And now these three remain: faith, hope and love.
But the greatest of these is love.
—1 *Corinthians* 13:13

Chapter One

"Sit." Kate Nichols took one look at her best friend's face and pointed to an empty booth by the window. "I'll be right back with a piece of pie."

"Just bring the whole thing." Abby Porter's sigh stirred the wisps of honey-blond hair on her forehead. "And a fork."

Kate shot her a sympathetic look. "That bad, huh?"

"Let's put it this way—for the past twenty-four hours I've been seriously contemplating a destination wedding," Abby said darkly.

"Mmm. Could be fun," Kate mused. "What's the destination?"

"Oh, possibly a tent in the middle of the

Sahara. Maybe a remote tropical island." Abby's silver-green eyes narrowed. *"Jupiter."*

Kate tried not to smile as she retrieved a piece of triple berry pie from the revolving dessert case near the cash register and topped it with a scoop of vanilla ice cream.

She set the plate and a carafe of fresh coffee down on the table in front of Abby before sliding into the opposite side of the booth. "Interesting choices but I'm not sure I see a pattern. What's the criteria?"

"There's only one," Abby admitted as she attacked the pie. "Somewhere my brother can't find me."

Kate suppressed a smile. "I hate to be the one who breaks this to you, but I'm pretty sure the 'tent in the Sahara' thing won't work."

"Why not?"

"Because Alex probably holds stock in some high-tech spy satellite. He'd track you down in no time."

Abby frowned as she considered that. "Scratch that one, then. Tropical island?"

"Definitely a no go unless you're willing to choose a new maid of honor. My hair and humidity are sworn enemies." To prove her point, Kate tweaked a flame-colored curl that seemed to have doubled in size since she'd unlocked the door of the Grapevine Café at six o'clock that morning. "Not to mention that Alex has a yacht."

"You're right." The words tumbled out with Abby's sigh. "I guess that leaves Jupiter."

"Uh-uh." Kate leaned forward and lowered her voice a notch. "He owns it."

"Kate!" Abby choked back a laugh.

Kate simply looked at her.

"Okay, because there's a slight—very slight, mind you—chance that you're right, I'll take Jupiter off the list, too," Abby grumbled.

"And several other planets in the solar system," Kate said under her breath.

They shared a grin.

"All right." Abby gave up. "It looks like I'm back to where I started. Getting married at the inn."

Which was, Kate knew, exactly the place that Abby and her fiancé, Quinn O'Halloran, wanted to exchange their vows.

Shortly after the couple announced their

engagement, Alex Porter had done his best to persuade Abby to hold the wedding in the grand ballroom of a swanky Chicago hotel. One of—count them—four swanky hotels the Porter family happened to *own* in the midwest.

It was clear the wealthy executive didn't think that a small ceremony and outdoor reception were good enough for his only sibling.

If she were Abby, Kate would be contemplating Jupiter, too. Either that or sending the guy on a one-way trip to the moon.

Not, Kate thought, that it would do any good. The man possessed both the ways and means to find his way back.

Alex Porter was nothing if not…resourceful. Creatively, ingeniously and, yes, sometimes even scarily resourceful.

He'd proven that the previous summer when he'd secretly hired Quinn O'Halloran, a local security systems expert and former bodyguard, to keep an eye on Abby when she'd moved to Mirror Lake.

Kate had found out the whole story after she and Abby became friends. How Alex had hoped his sister would give up what he considered to be a foolish dream—turning an old Bible camp on the lake into a bed-and-breakfast—and return to Chicago where she belonged. How the plan had backfired when Abby and Quinn fell in love.

Abby had patiently held her ground over the past few months when her brother made his opinions known, but Kate had doled out enough slices of pie to know it wasn't always easy. For all Alex Porter's bossy ways, the two siblings were close and Abby hated to be at odds with him. In spite of their obvious differences, Abby talked about her older brother with exasperated but genuine affection.

Kate totally understood the exasperation. The affection, not so much.

Secretly, she figured the bond between them had more to do with Abby's sweet, generous nature and her strong faith rather than some unseen quality that might lay buried like a vein of gold in the heart that beat beneath Alex Porter's Armani suit.

"So what is big brother's problem now?" Kate asked as she filled two coffee mugs to the brim. "The wedding is less than a week away. There can't be anything left at risk for a hostile takeover."

"You'd be surprised," Abby muttered.

Kate silently scrolled through the list of wedding details she knew Alex had taken issue with. "Is he still upset that Jessica and Tony will be running the inn while you're gone?"

"It was hard for Alex to give up one of his favorite managers *and* head pastry chef for two weeks, but he hasn't said anything about that for a while. Probably because he knows they'll do a great job." Abby smiled. "Jessica plans to cut back to part-time until she has the baby but she insists that taking over my kitchen will feel like a vacation. And Tony is hoping to do a little fishing when he isn't manning the desk."

"So Tony and Jessica are safe." Relieved, Kate mentally crossed that one off her list and went onto the next one. "He doesn't approve of your decision to carry a bouquet of wildflowers so he hired his personal florist to change your mind?"

"He doesn't have a..." Abby paused. "Never

mind. But, no, I'm happy to report that my Queen Anne's lace and daisies are safe at the moment."

"So what is it now?"

"He thinks…oh, it doesn't matter." To Kate's astonishment, Abby's smile faded and she averted her gaze. "You know Alex."

Kate didn't. Not really. She had only met the man once, a year ago, when he'd driven up in a silver Viper to check on Abby and make one last-ditch effort to convince her to leave Mirror Lake.

But because Abby talked about her brother a lot, Kate *felt* as if she knew him. And what she knew—other than the fact that Alex Porter oozed confidence out of every pore and happened to be quite unfairly, in Kate's opinion, drop-dead gorgeous—didn't impress her very much. As far as she was concerned, Alex tried to control peoples' lives the same way he did his hotels. With a lift of one autocratic eyebrow. That it seemed to work for the guy was another cause for irritation.

"Well, he must have said something or you

wouldn't be threatening to elope five days before your wedding," Kate pointed out.

"It's nothing to be concerned about, really. Alex had some…questions…about the reception dinner," Abby finally admitted.

"It's all set. You and Quinn approved the menu. I have everything ready…" Kate stopped. Something in Abby's expression set off warning bells in her head.

Alex Porter didn't have questions. He had *doubts*. Doubts that a woman who operated a small café had the ability to cater his sister's wedding reception.

"He doesn't think I can do it." Kate wasn't sure why, but the thought stung.

"That's not it," Abby said quickly. "Alex just wondered whether you had the time to act as my maid of honor and handle the food for the reception."

No doubt he wondered more than that, Kate thought grimly. But just because the Porter hotels boasted award-winning restaurants didn't mean they were the only ones capable of creating a memorable reception dinner.

"I told Alex that I trust you completely," Abby continued. "Not only are you the queen of multitasking, you're a wonderful cook."

Kate was touched by her friend's loyalty, but Alex's assumption still rankled. She was forced to take her own advice when it came to dealing with stressful situations.

Keep your sense of humor.

"So what does he think is on the menu? Hamburgers and French fries?" Kate even managed a weak laugh.

Abby joined in. Sort of.

Kate's mouth dropped open. "He thinks that all I'm capable of making are hamburgers and French fries?"

"Not really," Abby murmured. Unfortunately, the look in her eyes flashed the words "yes, really."

Kate could *feel* the freckles on the bridge of her nose start to glow. "He thinks the Grapevine is a greasy spoon."

"It doesn't matter what Alex thinks." Abby's chin lifted. "He's never eaten at the café."

So, yes! A greasy spoon!

"I told him that you've won awards at the

county fair..." Kate stifled a groan. She knew her friend meant well, but a first-place ribbon for her triple berry pie and sour apple salsa wasn't going to impress someone like Alex. "...and just because the café is small, it doesn't mean that you deep-fry everything and sling hash—"

"Hash?" Kate squawked.

"Maybe he didn't say hash." Abby bit her lip.

The familiar gesture, the one Kate saw whenever Abby was trying to find a tactful way to say something—or *not* to say something—only led to one conclusion.

He'd said hash.

Abby must have recognized the look on her face. "Don't change your mind about catering the reception," she pleaded. "Alex will eat everything you prepare, and he'll love it. I promise."

The corners of Kate's lips curved in a slow smile. "Oh, don't worry. I'm not going to change my mind."

Because Alex Porter *would* eat everything she prepared for the reception dinner...and a generous helping of crow, as well.

* * *

Play nice.

Those were Abby's orders.

But Alex had found a loophole. His sister had been talking about her wedding day. If he arrived in town a few days early, technically those orders hadn't taken effect yet.

The truth was, Alex Porter didn't particularly care for orders unless *he* was the one giving them. And he didn't care for orders issued by his kid sister, either.

Not, Alex grudgingly admitted to himself, that Abby was a kid. Not anymore. But it was hard not to think of her as the fragile, introverted girl he'd single-handedly raised after their parents died while returning home from a business trip.

One phone call from a sheriff's deputy that night had changed the course of Alex's life. At the age of twenty-two and six weeks shy of obtaining his bachelor's degree, he had inherited the family estate, two hotels and the guardianship of his fourteen-year-old sister.

After the funeral, an attorney recommended that Alex "liquidate all the assets" in order to "disengage from the weighty responsibilities" that had been placed on him. Alex interpreted the 'liquidating of all assets' as polite legalese for disposing of the two hotels his parents had poured twenty years of their blood, sweat and tears into making a success. The "weighty responsibilities?" His only sibling.

He had dismissed the lawyer's advice. And the lawyer.

There'd been little time to grieve as he took charge of the business and Abby, the only other remaining member of the Porter family. Over the years, Alex had done everything in his power to protect them both.

That's why Abby's decision to walk away from the family business—and, if Alex were completely honest, from *him*—the previous summer had been a difficult one to accept.

Alex realized now that he should have taken his sister a little more seriously when she claimed she had to follow God's plan for her life. Whatever that meant. It was fine with him if people chose to look to God for direction, but Alex preferred to make his own plans.

But because he hadn't paid attention, Abby had decided to follow the old adage "actions speak louder than words" to prove her point. A point Alex still thought she could have made without turning in her letter of resignation and buying a run-down lodge in northern Wisconsin.

He figured that Abby would get married one day, but he'd always assumed he would have a little more...input...about the details. Like *who* she married. And when. And where.

At the very least, he assumed she would agree to hold the ceremony in Porter Lakeside's grand ballroom, surrounded by friends who moved within their social circle. But no. Abby had insisted on a simple wedding at the inn she'd opened; the guest list comprised a small group of people Alex didn't even know.

His fingers tightened around the leather steering wheel as a gap suddenly opened in the wall of trees and revealed the small town his sister now considered home.

Mirror Lake.

There was nothing special about the place that he could see. Certainly nothing special enough to tempt a person to turn their back on everything the Windy City had to offer.

He cruised down the narrow, paved walkway called Main Street. The large pots of marigolds stationed at the foot of each streetlamp must have been part of a community beautification project of some kind.

Too bad it had failed.

A hardware store with hand-printed signs in the window advertised a two-for-one sale on garden hoses. Alex shook his head. Hadn't these people heard of underground sprinkler systems? Next door, the plate glass windows of the variety store proudly displayed a blinding array of cheap sun catchers.

Alex decided it would serve Abby right if she received a dozen of the things as wedding gifts.

His gaze shifted to the third brick building in the lineup and snagged on a faded sign above the door.

The Grapevine Café.

Jerking the Viper to the right, Alex's foot tapped the brake so the vehicle wouldn't jump the curb and take out a pot of marigolds.

He cut the engine and stared at the old-fashioned diner in disbelief. Call him crazy, but for some reason, he'd pictured something with a little more curbside appeal. Something a little...bigger.

"What are you thinking, Abby?" he muttered. This was taking her friendship with the owner of the café—Kate Nichols—too far.

A memory, one that had lodged deep in his subconscious like a splinter, shifted and poked him again.

Almost a year ago, when he'd shown up at Abby's bed-and-breakfast to make one final appeal for her to come home, he'd walked right into the middle of a renovation party. Alex had confronted the first person he saw—a young woman with a cap of flame-colored curls and eyes as green as a field of fresh clover—and asked where he could find Abby. Instead of taking him to his sister, the pixie had had the audacity to lead him to a dilapidated cabin down by the lake instead. Then she'd pressed a hammer into his hand, pointed to the roof and told him to "make himself useful."

He hadn't appreciated being told what to do. Especially by a petite, redheaded firecracker.

Alex had tried to put her out of his mind but that wasn't easy when the name Kate Nichols popped up with annoying frequency during his phone conversations with Abby.

Business wouldn't exactly be booming for the owner of a café in a town the size of Mirror Lake. If he knew his tender-hearted sister, Abby had felt sorry for Kate, put aside her misgivings and hired her to cater the reception dinner. It might explain the strain he'd heard in Abby's voice when they had gone over the details for the reception the day before. Even with the simple wedding she was insisting upon, resources had to be limited.

Alex's eyes narrowed on a tear in the striped awning that shaded the sidewalk.

Very limited.

He got out of the car and reached the door in two strides. According to a piece of cardboard taped to the window, the café opened for business at six o'clock.

Alex glanced at the TAG Heuer on his wrist.

Two minutes past six.

Great. He'd be the first customer of the day.

Chapter Two

The bells over the front door jingled as Kate piped neat rows of whipped cream over the top of a fresh strawberry rhubarb pie.

"Find a place to sit and I'll be right with…"

You.

Kate felt a sudden disconnect between her brain and her voice when she spotted the man standing just inside the entrance, backlit by the early morning sun.

Alex Porter, in the flesh.

In *her* café.

She'd sat right next to Abby in church the day before and her friend hadn't warned— *told*—her that Alex would be in Mirror Lake.

A week early.

Their eyes met over the counter and Kate's heart did a backflip. As impossible as it seemed, the man was even more good-looking than she remembered.

She could see traces of Abby in the straight nose and high, smooth forehead, but the resemblance between the siblings ended there. Abby's silver-green eyes were warm, as if lit from within. A smile always played at the corner of her lips, ready to bloom at a moment's notice.

Alex's features, on the other hand, looked as if they'd been chiseled from a hunk of granite. His eyes were the same shade of green as the jade paperweight on Kate's desk. And just as cool. The fact that those eyes happened to be framed by ridiculously long lashes didn't count.

Not at all.

Short, windswept hair, toasted a light golden brown from the sun, made him look more suited to the deck of a sailboat than an office. The khaki pants and lightweight cotton shirt he wore looked casual enough but Kate wasn't fooled. Both looked as if they had been custom fit for his lean, muscular frame.

"Alex." Kate found her voice again. "What a surprise. I wasn't expecting to see you."

Until the wedding.

"Abby sounded a little stressed out the last time I talked to her." The rough velvet voice wielded an edge that immediately put Kate on the defensive. "I decided to drive up a few days early to help out."

Kate knew better. Men like Alex Porter didn't help out. They took over. And the guy probably didn't have a clue that *he* had been the cause of Abby's stress.

"Oh. Wonderful." Just wonderful. "Abby will be—" *insert tactful word here, Kate* "—surprised."

"Not for another hour or so." Alex's eyes narrowed when she didn't respond. "The café is open, right? So you don't mind if I sit down?"

"You want to eat here?" Kate blurted out.

Alex hesitated a split second too long. "Yes."

This is Abby's brother and she loves him, Kate reminded herself. For that reason and that reason only, she flashed one of her sunniest smiles. "You're the first customer of the day so go ahead and sit anywhere you like."

His gaze swept over the empty diner. In ten minutes she would be caught in the middle of the morning breakfast stampede; but judging from the skeptical look on his face, Alex doubted she would have another customer besides himself. All day.

Kate kept the smile pinned in place. "Would you like a cup of coffee?"

He gave a curt nod. "No cream or sugar."

Of course not. We wouldn't want to add something that might sweeten our disposition, now would we?

"No problem," Kate said out loud. "I'll be right back to take your order."

As Alex stalked to the back of the dining area to claim an empty lair, Kate retrieved a carafe from the coffee station. Her hands were actually trembling. Not out of fear but frustration. She couldn't believe that Abby shared the same DNA with this man.

Long lashes or not, Alex Porter was arrogant. Cold. Condescending.

And Kate knew exactly what had brought

him to the Grapevine. He wanted to see for himself what Mirror Lake's greasy spoon had to offer.

She searched her memory for an appropriate Scripture. One that would give her the self-control to pour the coffee into Alex's coffee cup, not over the top of his head.

Lord, I know there has to be one. Or one hundred. But I'm coming up empty at the moment. Sorry.

Kate set his coffee down and whipped the pen out of her apron pocket. Smile carefully balanced in place. "What can I get for you?"

Alex closed the menu with a decisive snap, as if there were nothing on the list of options that remotely tempted him. "I'll just have the special."

"Sure. Coming right up." Given the fact that she'd unlocked the door only moments before Alex made his appearance, Kate wasn't quite sure what the special of the day was.

Grady O'Rourke, the former military cook her father had hired when Kate was in first grade, took charge of the daily menu changes. When Kate had taken over the café, she and

Grady had amicably divided the kitchen duties. Grady claimed the griddle, Kate the stove.

She ducked around the counter. "I need a special, Grady."

"You got it." The man's off-key whistle accompanied the sizzle of butter in the cast-iron skillet.

Kate began to fill the dessert case with slices of the pies she'd made the night before, all too aware that a pair of jade-green eyes tracked her every movement.

"Order up, katydid," Grady bellowed.

Kate winced, hoping Alex hadn't heard the cook call her by the affectionate nickname he'd bestowed on her when she was six years old.

"Thanks." Kate grabbed the steaming plate on the pass-through and felt the blood drain from her face. "Grady?" The word came out in a squeak.

"Problem?"

"No…no problem." If a person didn't count the six-foot-tall, two-hundred-pound problem sitting at a booth in the back. "I don't think you've made this before."

"Nope." A smile bisected the grizzled face. "But mark my words. It'll be a big hit."

"I'm sure it will," Kate said faintly.

Most days, Grady's "special" came from a list of what he liked to call his "tried and trues." Steak and potatoes. Blueberry pancakes. Ham and cheese omelets.

Why, oh why, couldn't this have been one of those days?

Show no fear. Kate gave herself an internal pep talk as she breezed back to Alex's booth. "Here you go. Enjoy!"

His gaze dropped to the plate and bounced back up again. "What is this?"

"The special." Kate wished it hadn't come out sounding like a question.

Alex arched a brow.

In retaliation, Kate lifted her chin. "It's…a delicious blend of meat and potatoes with a hint of spice."

"I see," Alex said softly. "And does this delicious blend of meat and potatoes happen to have a *name?*"

Yes, it did. And he was going to make her say it.

"It's…hash." Kate pushed the word through gritted teeth.

The perfectly sculpted lips—Kate felt a trickle of horror that she noticed they *were* perfectly sculpted—curled at the edges.

"That's what I thought…katydid."

Organized chaos.

It was the only description that Alex could come up with to describe what he was seeing. Although it was possible that the word *organized* was too generous.

Total chaos would probably be more accurate.

He got dizzy just watching Kate Nichols in motion.

The woman fairly crackled with energy, making him wonder if the red curls poking out from beneath the floral bandana she wore doubled as some kind of power source.

In the space of half an hour, Kate had greeted each customer who came through the door by name. Paused to hug the blond, waiflike teenager who'd joined forces with her during the breakfast rush as if they were long-lost sisters. She'd even plucked a cranky toddler out of a portable highchair and balanced him on one slender hip while she rang up receipts so his weary young parents had an opportunity to finish their breakfast in peace.

Alex's blood pressure spiked when Kate joined a group of men at their table to referee a lively discussion about the number of potholes on Oak Street.

Kate's relaxed posture and easy laughter made him grit his teeth.

Didn't she realize how dangerous it was to get that close to people? To let them get that close to *you?*

His parents had learned a lesson on setting boundaries the hard way. Abby had been six years old when a disgruntled hotel employee abducted her. The police had found her a few days later, frightened but otherwise unharmed. The family physician who'd examined Abby had reassured them that her memory of the ordeal would fade in time.

Alex, who'd been a freshman in high school, hadn't been as lucky.

The three days Abby went missing remained etched in his mind. So had the days that followed her safe return. Their parents enrolled them in private school. His and Abby's lives became governed by a set of rules that formed a barrier around them as impenetrable as the walls surrounding the Porter estate.

It was one of the reasons Alex had become so protective of his sister over the years. They'd lost their parents—he wasn't about to lose the only remaining member of his family.

Kate might not realize it, but she was asking for trouble. Her smile was too friendly. Too engaging…

"Would you like a refill?"

Alex looked up and silently amended his opinion. Kate's smile was engaging unless it was directed at him. Then it cooled to the temperature of day-old coffee. But he hadn't come to Mirror Lake to make friends—he'd come walk his baby sister down the aisle. And to make sure there were no unexpected bumps along the way. From what he'd witnessed so far, putting Kate Nichols in charge of something as important as Abby's wedding reception would guarantee more bumps than Oak Street had potholes.

"No thanks."

"You're ready for the bill?"

"Not yet." With two simple words, Alex managed to extinguish the hopeful look in those clover-green eyes.

"All right." He could almost *see* her silently counting to five...no, ten. For some reason, Alex found a perverse satisfaction in knowing he got under her skin, too.

"Kate?" The teenage waitress sidled up. "Mr. Dinsman ordered the biscuits and gravy," she whispered.

"Absolutely not, Missy." Kate shook her head, setting the corkscrew curls into motion. "I know what his cholesterol is. The only thing on the menu for Mr. Dinsman is a bowl of oatmeal."

The waitress chewed on her lower lip. "He said that if you make him eat oatmeal, he won't leave a tip."

"Well, here's a tip for *him,*" Kate said tartly. "If he wants to clog his arteries, he should stay home and make his own breakfast."

Missy glanced at the portly man who sat a

few tables away, glowering in their direction. "Do I have to tell him that?"

"No, sprinkle some fresh blueberries on the oatmeal and tell him there's no charge." Kate winked at her. "That'll make the fiber go down easier."

"Okay." Missy grinned before darting away.

Alex had to ask. He just had to. "You know a customer's cholesterol level?"

"It's a small town—and a very small café." Kate sounded proud of the fact rather than apologetic.

"Kate!" A man with a flowing white beard and brows that resembled an unclipped hedge waved a folder stuffed full of papers at her. "When you have a minute, can you look over the minutes from the last city council meeting?"

Kate didn't seem at all surprised by the request. "I'll be right there, Mayor Dodd."

"You should hire more help." Alex had to raise his voice a notch to make himself heard over the steady hum of conversation.

The watercolor pink lips compressed. "I appreciate your concern—" judging from her tone, Alex doubted that was true "—but I do all right."

"Really?" He watched a gray-haired man shuffle around the cash register and select a tall parfait glass from the shelf. "Maybe if you had more help, your customers wouldn't be forced to sneak behind the counter to make their own food."

Kate followed the direction of his gaze and Alex heard a soft but audible chirp of dismay.

"Excuse me." She shot away, the tails of her canvas apron streaming behind her like kite ribbons.

A trio of women trundled past Alex in a cloud of perfume, the scents clashing like the instruments in an amateur marching band. They crowded around into the booth next to his and began to pull out their knitting.

Knitting.

The dining area reminded him of a noisy family gathering. A limp copy of the local newspaper passed from table to table as if following some kind of prearranged system. Children hung over the backs of the booths and people roamed around the room, chatting or blatantly eavesdropping on the conversations going on around them.

He couldn't help but compare the Grapevine to the restaurants in his hotels. Soft background music. A well-trained wait staff who'd memorized the selections on the menu but remained blissfully unaware of a customer's cholesterol level. High-backed leather booths that provided peace, quiet and...

"Good morning." Abby slipped into a chair across from him.

Anonymity.

"How did you find me?"

His sister didn't look at all intimidated by his scowl. "Someone called me and said you were here, scaring the customers."

Alex had a hunch he knew who'd called. But when had she found the time between taking orders, babysitting crabby toddlers and refereeing that lively debate over who was responsible for repairing the potholes on Oak Street?

"I'm not scaring anyone. I'm having breakfast."

"Yes." Abby cleared her throat. "That's why it's a little strange that you ended up here, given the fact that your sister runs a bed-and-*breakfast*."

"I got into town a little early—" *Four* days, he thought he heard Abby say under her breath. "And I didn't want to disturb you."

"Since when?"

Alex ignored that as he got a bead on Kate again. Instead of shooing the elderly man back to his table, she had retreated to the kitchen, leaving him alone with the blender. An accident—and a lawsuit—waiting to happen.

"Come on. I'm taking you back to the inn." Abby stood up. "And leave Kate a big tip. I'm sure she earned it."

"I already did. I told her that she needed to hire more help." Alex left the money he owed on the table and rose to his feet.

"Really?" Abby shook her head. "I'm surprised you lived to tell about it."

Alex remembered the spark of emerald fire in Kate's eyes and clamped down on a smile. "There were witnesses."

"Leave Kate alone," his sister commanded. "She doesn't need your advice. She took over the café when she was twenty years old. Most people that age are still trying to figure out what to do with their lives."

"She tries to be in three different places at once." He'd almost suffered an attack of vertigo just watching her.

"Kate has everything under control." Abby tucked her arm through his and herded him out the door with impressive speed. "You of all people should appreciate the quality."

He ignored that, too. "Under control? If that were true, her customers wouldn't have to make their own food."

Abby frowned. "What are you talking about?"

"The man behind the counter. I saw him making a milkshake."

Understanding dawned in Abby's eyes.

"It was probably Arthur Lundy," she explained. "His wife, Marsha, died last year and now he's in the early stages of Alzheimer's. According to Kate, they grew up in Mirror Lake. He proposed to Marsha right there at the soda fountain while they shared a milkshake.

"Some days Mr. Lundy comes into the café and he doesn't seem to remember that she's gone. He'll go behind the counter to make a milkshake and ask for two straws. Kate doesn't mind."

His sister's tone suggested that he shouldn't, either.

"This is a business, not a home," Alex said, capping off some unidentifiable emotion that bubbled to the surface of his conscience. "It's a mistake to let the customers do as they please. She's responsible if one of them gets hurt."

"Kate looks at people like Mr. Lundy as more than just a customer."

Alex's lips twisted.

"That's mistake number two."

Chapter Three

Mission accomplished.

With a satisfied smile, Kate tacked down the last string of white lights along the roofline of the gazebo. When Quinn and Abby returned from their final premarital counseling session with Matthew Wilde, the pastor at Church of the Pines, they would discover the garden area transformed into a wonderland of fragrant blooms and twinkling lights.

She scooted away from the edge of the roof, careful not to look at the ten-foot drop to the flagstone patio below. Kate didn't particularly care for heights but decorating for the reception was a labor of love for her friends.

And because stringing lights around the gazebo had been her idea to begin with, she didn't think it was fair to ask someone else to put them up.

Hammer tucked under her arm, Kate swung a foot onto the top rung of the ladder. A sudden commotion had her twisting around just in time to see Mulligan and Lady, Quinn and Abby's dogs, race around the corner of the lodge. Both animals were linked together by the long rope clamped between their jaws. And they were heading in her direction.

Kate swiftly calculated destination, speed and distance and threw herself back onto the roof. A split second later, Lady ducked under the ladder while Mulligan veered to the right. The rope went through the middle. It was Kate's foot, however, that connected with the top of the ladder, which teetered back and forth before it hit the ground with an impressive crash.

Leaving her stranded.

Kate groaned. "Now what am I supposed to do?" she called down.

The dogs, who circled back to survey the

damage, looked at each other. Kate was pretty sure she saw them shrug.

She rose cautiously to her feet and looked around. There was no sign of Abby's guests taking a leisurely walk by the lake. Kate checked the pockets of her cargo shorts before remembering that she'd left her cell phone in a safe place—on the wicker table in the gazebo.

Maybe she could jump. It didn't look that *far* down.

She peeked over the edge and swallowed hard.

It was that far down.

There was only one thing to do. Pray for a quick rescue by a good Samaritan—or that Abby and Quinn would return sooner than expected.

"Either one, Lord," she murmured. "I'm flexible."

At least she didn't have to worry about Alex discovering her in this predicament. Abby had mentioned that her brother had made plans to meet with Jeff Gaines, a local developer and kindred millionaire, and wouldn't be back until later that night.

Another twenty minutes crawled by. The setting sun melted into the trees, but Kate couldn't even appreciate the way it turned the lake to liquid gold. She was too busy fending off the swarm of mosquitoes that had found an easy target.

Just when Kate was contemplating how soft a landing the bed of hydrangeas would provide, Lady launched to her feet and shot down the path, releasing a chain of sharp little barks. A canine SOS.

Kate's relief turned to dismay when she heard the low rumble of a masculine voice. A *familiar* masculine voice.

She wondered if it was too late to add an addendum to her earlier prayer. Because Alex Porter was the last person she wanted to come to her rescue.

Out of the corner of his eye, Alex saw two furry missiles hurtling toward him. One was Mulligan, the walking carpet that Abby insisted on calling a dog; the other a buff-colored cocker spaniel he assumed belonged to Quinn. Both animals performed figure eights around his feet, voices raised in a duet that threatened to pierce his eardrums.

Alex winced. "That's enough, you two. Time to go inside. You're disturbing the peace." More specifically, *his* peace.

As he bent down to take hold of Lady's collar, the dog danced out of reach and trotted up the path. Every few feet she would stop, glance over her shoulder and bark. Between each little yip, Mulligan interjected a mournful howl of his own.

"Quiet!"

In the split second of silence that followed Alex's command, he thought he heard something that sounded suspiciously like a... groan.

Frowning, Alex strode down the narrow flagstone path that wove through the gardens and opened into a spacious patio area. There was no one there. But next to the old-fashioned gazebo, he spotted a ladder lying on its side and a rope tangled around one of the legs.

"I get it." Alex shook his head. "Okay, now that we've returned to the scene of the crime, which one of you knocked it over?"

Mulligan barked twice. And looked up.

Before he realized what he was doing, Alex did, too.

He blinked, wondering if the evening shadows were playing tricks on him. But no…it was her. The very woman who'd been plaguing his thoughts for the past twenty-four hours was perched on the roof of the gazebo.

"What," Alex said, "are you doing up there?"

"Waiting for a helicopter," Kate said promptly.

"Landing might be a bit of a challenge." A smile rustled at the corner of Alex's lips as he went to pick up the ladder. "In the meantime, would you like some help?"

Absolute silence greeted the question.

Alex realized that Kate was actually *thinking* about it. Instead of being offended, he was overcome with a sudden urge to laugh.

"All right." She stood up and inched her way over to the edge of the roof while Alex repositioned the ladder next to the gazebo. As Kate scampered down, he reached out and took hold of her arm in an attempt to steady her. The contact with her bare skin created a jolt of awareness that made Alex feel as if he'd been branded.

He released her immediately and Kate stumbled back. "Thank you," she muttered.

Noticing the flush on her cheeks, Alex frowned. "How long were you up there?"

"Thirteen."

"Minutes?"

"No. Mosquito bites." Kate scratched behind her ear and sighed. "Make that fourteen."

Alex tamped down another smile. "Now are you going to tell me what you were doing up there?"

"I'll show you instead." Kate disappeared into the gazebo and dozens of white lights illuminated the entire structure. She popped back up in the doorway a moment later. "What do you think?"

"I think you're going to attract every flying insect for a five-mile radius."

Kate didn't appear at all fazed by his observation. "I already thought of that. There will be citronella candles strategically placed around the garden during the reception."

"The reception is going to be here?"

Her eyes widened. "Didn't Abby mention that?"

"No, but that doesn't surprise me." Alex had offered to help with the planning on several occasions, but Abby had resisted all his suggestions. Frustrated, he'd asked if there was anything he *would* be allowed to do. That's when his sister had finally given him a task.

You can give me away.

Alex felt his throat tighten at the memory.

It was the one thing he wasn't sure he would be able to do when the time came.

As the silence stretched between them, Kate released a slow breath.

She hadn't expected applause but something other than a scowl would have been nice. "You don't approve of an outdoor reception?" she guessed.

"It's not that I don't approve," Alex said, his voice tight with something that sounded a lot like disapproval.

"Then what is it?"

Alex appeared taken aback by the question. Maybe because, Kate acknowledged ruefully, he wasn't used to being questioned!

"This wedding wasn't the kind that I envisioned for Abby," he said after a moment. "I thought every woman wanted a fairy-tale wedding. The big puffy dress. Dozens of roses—"

"A horse-drawn carriage. String quartet," Kate murmured.

Alex's eyebrows shot up and she cringed. Finishing people's sentences was one of her worst habits! And Kate could only hope Alex wouldn't realize that what she'd described was *her* dream wedding, not Abby's.

"Some women dream of all that," she said quickly. "But Abby likes things simple, you know."

"I'll have to take your word for that," Alex said. A shadow passed across his face, so fleeting that Kate wondered if she'd imagined it. "I practically raised her, but she's changed since she moved to Mirror Lake."

The changes in her friend had more to do with her relationship with God than a change of scenery; but Kate wasn't sure Alex would understand. According to Abby, he remained openly skeptical about her faith.

"I caught her spying on a wedding at one of the hotels when she was about fifteen," Alex said, his voice so low that it was almost as if he were speaking to himself. "It was the event of the summer. Ice sculptures. Fresh flowers flown in from Hawaii. I saw the look on Abby's face when the bride and groom came in and I decided that when she got married, even though our parents couldn't be there to make things perfect for her, I could."

As Kate listened, it occurred to her that she hadn't thought about the situation from Alex's point of view until now. Abby had been in her teens when their parents died. Alex wasn't simply an older brother smiling from the sidelines as he watched his sister get married. It was more complicated than that.

I practically raised her.

"The wedding will be special for Abby," Kate ventured. "Her close friends and family will be there. You'll walk her down the aisle where Quinn will be waiting. Those are the things that matter the most to her."

"It just seems like there should be...more," Alex said. "It should be perfect."

"This *is* Abby's more—and that means it's perfect," Kate said.

Alex stared at her and the look in his eyes

made Kate catch her breath. Because this Alex Porter, the one who appeared…uncertain…was infinitely more dangerous than the millionaire CEO who insisted on having his own way.

He opened his mouth to say something but didn't get the opportunity because the approach of a car drew the dogs' attention. Lady took off down the stone path while Mulligan chose a shortcut through the bushes.

"It sounds like they're back." Kate followed Lady, aware that Alex was right behind her.

Quinn had parked the car and was opening the passenger door for Abby when they stepped into the driveway. The moment her friend got out, Kate could tell that something was wrong. Alex saw it, too.

"Abby?" His brows dipped together in a frown. "What happened?"

In a silent appeal, Abby looked at her fiancé. Quinn clasped her hand, his expression grim. "We should talk inside."

As if by silent agreement, everyone trooped inside and headed straight for the kitchen. Abby went over to the sink and began to fill the teakettle with water. When she turned back again, Kate didn't miss the glaze of unshed tears in her friend's eyes.

"Jessica called when Quinn and I were on our way here," Abby began. "She had an appointment with her OB doctor this afternoon and he found symptoms of a condition called preeclampsia. To be safe, he put her on complete bed rest for the next few months."

"The next few months?" Kate echoed. "But that means she and Tony won't be able to attend the wedding on Saturday!"

Abby leaned against Quinn and his arms immediately came around her, bracketing her slender frame. "I'm afraid not."

"Oh, Abby." Kate's heart wrenched at the thought of the couple missing out on such a special day. Jessica and Tony Benson had been instrumental in leading Abby to the Lord and she counted them among her closest friends. "I know how important it was to have them here."

Alex shot her a grim look. "That's not all it means," he pointed out. "They won't be able to take over the inn while you go on your honeymoon, either."

"What's important is Jessica and the baby's

health," Abby said softly. "If it means delaying our honeymoon trip for a little while, then that's what we'll have to do."

Quinn nodded. "We already prayed about it and we trust that God is in control of the situation."

Kate felt the sting of tears in her own eyes. Before he'd met Abby, Quinn had been angry at the world—and God. "You're right. He knows what you need."

"So do I," Alex said. "You need a temporary manager. I can take over while you're gone."

Three pairs of eyes turned to him in amazement.

"You?" Quinn was the only one brave enough to voice the question.

"Don't look so surprised. I do own four hotels," Alex reminded his future brother-in-law.

The couple exchanged a look.

"But this is a bed-and-*breakfast*," Abby said.

"Your point?" The eyebrow lifted.

"You don't know how to cook," Quinn said bluntly.

To Kate's astonishment, Alex didn't deny
it. She glanced at Abby and found herself on
the receiving end of a bright smile.

Oh, no.

Kate could read her friend's mind. Now she
could only hope that Abby could read hers.

Don't say it, Abby.

But Abby did say it. Out loud.

"Kate does."

Chapter Four

"What?"

"What!"

The words collided in midair. Alex's came out like a pistol shot while Kate's was just as loud but sounded more like a…oh, let's be honest…a *squeak*.

"Alex knows how to run a hotel and you know how to run a kitchen." Abby's gaze bounced between Kate and Alex, as if daring them to disagree. "It makes perfect sense."

Kate swallowed a groan. How could she say no to her best friend? But following that line of reasoning, how could her best friend expect her to work alongside a man who assumed her main culinary achievement was corned beef hash?

It wasn't that Kate didn't want to come to Quinn and Abby's rescue. She did. But that didn't mean she wanted to share a lifeboat with Alex Porter!

Kate reached for an excuse. Any excuse.

"I'm not sure Grady can manage without me," she stammered, silently apologizing to her cook, who had fed platoons of hungry soldiers for years. "And I don't have Alex's minions to call on for help."

"Did you," Alex said softly, "just use the word minions?"

"It's the only one that fit," Kate admitted.

Quinn clapped his hand over his mouth to stifle a sudden coughing fit.

"You're right, Kate." Abby mustered a brave smile. "Half the town depends on you, not just Grady. It isn't fair to ask you to split your time between here and the café. The inn offers a full breakfast every morning in addition to afternoon tea once a week. You wouldn't have a minute to yourself."

Kate should have been relieved that Abby had let her off the hook so easily, but all she felt was guilt.

"Don't worry, Abby." Alex muscled his

way back into the conversation. "I'll reassign a real…" He caught himself. "A chef from one of the hotels.

"I'm sure given the right incentive, I can convince one of my—" He paused and stared down at Kate with a glint in his eyes, as if he knew she was silently filling in the blank with the word "minions." "—*employees* to take your place for two weeks."

Some of the worry lifted from Abby's eyes but not all of it.

And Kate knew why. Alex's "right incentive" translated into the right amount of numbers added to someone's weekly paycheck.

Kate chewed on her lower lip. She and Abby had more in common than their faith and a love for the community they called home. They understood what it meant to be the sole owner of a business. For Abby to leave her kitchen in the hands of a stranger was the equivalent of leaving a beloved child in the care of a babysitter rather than a trusted friend or family member.

In this situation, Abby had both—if Kate could put aside her misgivings about working closely with Alex.

Kate drew in a breath and released it with a silent prayer.

We can do it for two weeks, can't we, Lord?

"I'll talk to Grady," she said. "The café closes at two every day. That should give me plenty of time to drive over to the inn and get a head start on breakfast for the next day. Thursday is my day off, so that's when I'll host the afternoon tea."

"Really?" A smile bloomed on Abby's face. "Are you sure? I know it's asking a lot."

"Missy is leaving for college at the end of the month and she's been asking for more hours. She might be willing to open right away in the morning and as long as I keep up with the baking, Grady can handle the kitchen."

The more Kate thought about it, the more she realized it *could* work.

Until the harbinger of doom spoke up.

"I still think you should let me hire a chef, Abby. Like you said, Kate has a lot of responsibilities—"

"None of which are more important than you and Quinn," Kate interjected.

Alex cut her a look cool enough to flash-freeze a package of pork chops. "Do you realize you have a tendency to finish other people's sentences?"

"Oh, yes." For once Kate didn't feel the need to apologize. "It's a habit."

"It's also—"

"One of the things we love about Kate," Quinn said smoothly before Alex could insult his new business partner.

The jade eyes narrowed on his future brother-in-law. "You just did it, too."

"Only to avoid bloodshed," Quinn murmured.

Kate found it interesting that no one had to ask what he meant.

"So, this is great." Abby stepped from the shelter of Quinn's arms to pull her brother into a hug. With her free hand, she motioned to Kate.

No, Abby! Not a group hug...

Kate gulped as Abby reeled her in, briefly linking the three of them together. For a moment, Kate's shoulder brushed against Alex's and the hint of lime in his cologne caused her traitorous nose to twitch in appreciation.

"You guys are amazing," Abby murmured. "I won't worry about a thing. Not with Alex managing the office and Kate in the kitchen."

"And a line of yellow police tape strung up between the two," Quinn murmured.

Kate made a face at him over Abby's shoulder before she wriggled free.

"That means I'll be running the day-to-day operations," Alex said. "Handling reservations. Overseeing the staff. The hiring and the firing."

"You won't have to fire anyone." Abby frowned at her brother.

"Of course not," Alex said in that crushed velvet voice. "I just wanted to make sure I understood."

He took a step away from Abby and smiled. At her.

Suddenly, Kate understood, too.

She might be in charge of the kitchen, but Alex was in charge of the inn in which that particular kitchen resided. Meaning that he was in charge of *her.*

Like it or not, she had just become one of Alex Porter's minions.

* * *

"Are you listening to me, Alex?"

Alex jerked to attention, upsetting Mulligan, who had camped out at his feet in the gathering room. "I always listen to you."

They both knew it wasn't true but Abby gave him a patient look.

"I know you think that taking care of the inn for two weeks is going to be easy, but it will definitely have its share of challenges."

Challenges. That about summed it up, Alex thought.

"I'm sure we'll get along fine." As long as Kate Nichols stuck to making tea, blueberry muffins and dainty finger sandwiches.

Quinn and Kate had left the inn over an hour ago, but Alex could *still* smell her perfume. Of course the woman wouldn't choose something tame, like vanilla. No, she wore a stirring, heady scent that reminded him of the tangle of plumeria that grew outside the door of his condo in Hawaii.

He realized Abby was staring at him.

"What are you talking about?"

"What are *you* talking about?" he shot back.

"I'm talking about the challenges of running a small bed-and-breakfast…" Understanding dawned in Abby's eyes. "You were talking about Kate, weren't you?"

Alex avoided the question. "I don't understand why you won't let me bring in a professional."

Abby shot him an exasperated look. "Kate *is* a professional. She's one of the most respected business owners in Mirror Lake—" As if anticipating his reaction to that, she raised her hand like a crossing guard. "If you don't trust her, at least trust me. I wouldn't have asked Kate for help if I didn't believe she was capable."

"Capable isn't always enough," Alex said. "You know the Porter family motto."

"Don't tell me you still…" Abby paused. "Never mind. Of course I remember it. You had the words engraved on a plaque for my high school graduation gift. 'Don't settle for anything but the best.'"

"So you see? It's not personal."

"It never is," Abby said softly. "Maybe that's the problem."

Not as far as Alex was concerned. He had rules in place for that sort of thing. Most of the people he came into contact with strove to keep their professional and personal lives separate. He'd come to the conclusion long ago that life ran much more smoothly if he kept his entire life professional. No blurred boundaries. Minimal conflict. It worked for him.

He thought it had been working for Abby, too, until she'd broken rank and moved to Mirror Lake.

"It's getting late." Alex eased his foot out from under Mulligan's bristly chin and rose to his feet. "Hopefully you'll see things my way in the morning."

"Is this a good time to mention that placing a tape recorder under a person's pillow and playing subliminal messages only works in the movies?"

"That's what you think."

Abby grinned. "Good night, bossy older brother."

"Good night, annoying little sister."

Just as he reached the door, one of the decorative sofa pillows smacked him in the back of the head. Alex caught the tasseled grenade before it hit the floor and lobbed it back.

"Does O'Halloran know about your temper?"

"Quinn calls it spunk." A hint of mischief stole into his sister's eyes. "I just wanted to tell you that I tweaked the Porter family motto a bit."

"That's it. I'm calling my attorney."

Abby ignored him. "Now I live by the motto 'Don't settle for anything but *God's* best.' And, in this case, that's exactly what I'm doing. Kate understands that what makes people repeat customers isn't only the food on the table, it's the feeling they get *at* the table."

Feelings?

Alex was pretty sure that 'feelings' didn't account for the success of the four hotels in the Porter chain. His guests returned because they wanted a professional staff waiting in the wings, poised to meet their every need—not a buddy.

An image of Kate, claiming an empty chair at the tableful of men who were discussing the dangerous potholes on Oak Street, came to mind. He would have fired her on the spot for that kind of familiarity.

"You don't know what I'm talking about, do you?"

"I know you've been spending too much time in the 'Kum ba yah' circle since you moved here."

Abby chuckled. "You're welcome to take my place at the campfire while Quinn and I are on our honeymoon. Kate can teach you the words."

The sarcastic comeback Alex was about to make was suddenly hijacked by a redheaded sprite.

This is Abby's more—and that means it's perfect.

He pushed the memory aside.

Learn something from Kate?

What did she know about 'more'? She lived in a backwoods town with a population of less than a thousand. The dining room of her café was smaller than the master bathroom in one of his suites.

Abby clucked her tongue. "I know that look, Alex."

"What look?"

"Don't sell Kate short. She's taught me a lot about friendship…and faith…since I've known her."

Then she definitely had nothing to teach him. Alex had closed the door on both those things a long time ago.

* * *

"Doug...you...*chicken!*"

The burly truck driver, who'd been filling out the inventory receipt, glowered at Kate. "Didn't Mrs. Carlson tell you not to call me names?"

"That was in second grade," Kate huffed. "And I didn't... I'm not calling you names! I'm talking about the chicken that was supposed to be on the truck today."

The chicken that was to serve as the main entrée for Abby and Quinn's wedding reception.

"It's there." Doug's platter-size palm thumped her gently on the head as if she were a golden retriever puppy. "I saw it."

Kate felt a headache sink its talons into the back of her skull. The café was the first stop on Doug's predawn run and she was glad she'd checked the order before he'd left. Most of the time, he unloaded the boxes straight into the walk-in freezer while she signed the paperwork.

But the past forty-eight hours, Kate had gotten a little paranoid.

One of the freezers had died two nights

ago, forcing her to dispose of half the inventory. Her best waitress had had a family emergency and Kate wasn't able to find a replacement on short notice. So instead of devoting precious hours on the prep work for the reception dinner, she'd had to wait tables instead.

To top it off, the '57 Thunderbird she'd inherited from her grandfather had thrown another temper tantrum and refused to leave the garage. To get from Point A to Point B, Kate had to make do with the canary-yellow Schwinn she'd received on her twelfth birthday.

And let's not forget that you and Alex Porter are about to become temporary business partners.

Kate suppressed a shudder. There was no denying it. The man managed to get under her skin—like a splinter. If she didn't know better, she might think he was responsible for all the obstacles that had been thrown into her path.

"I saw a box marked chicken," Doug said in a soothing voice. The voice a person used when talking to small children. And golden retriever puppies.

"What you saw was a box of frozen chicken *patties*." Kate's back teeth snapped together on the last word.

"So what's the fuss?"

"The *fuss*..." Kate cleared her throat to open a passage in which to breathe. "Is that I didn't order a box of frozen chicken patties. I ordered fresh, free-range chicken cut into kabob-size pieces."

"Huh." Doug scratched the back of his head. "That's weird."

"It's worse than weird, Doug. I need that chicken for Abby and Quinn's wedding reception. *Tomorrow*."

"Can't you just substitute? Nothing wrong with chicken patties. Smear 'em with a little mustard and—"

"I'm calling my supplier." Kate veered toward the oversize closet that passed for her office. "Don't leave," she called over her shoulder.

"I'm on a tight schedule today, Kate."

"Five minutes," she ground out. "Help yourself to coffee."

Doug's lips peeled back into a wide grin, unveiling a gold-capped incisor. "Okay."

Kate took two laps around the desk, debating whether it was too early to call the Jensens, who owned a small farm several miles from Mirror Lake. The couple had stopped in and introduced themselves early in the summer. Kate had never ordered from them before but she had a soft spot for family-owned businesses.

The first order she'd placed was for the meat and fresh produce for Abby and Quinn's wedding.

Farmers were up with the sunrise, weren't they?

Kate took a deep breath and dialed the number. Just when she was about to hang up, a young woman answered.

"North Star Organics. Amber Jensen speaking."

Kate took a deep breath, praying that once she explained the situation to Amber, the mistake would be rectified and all would be right with the world.

The absolute silence on the other end of the phone told her otherwise.

"I'm really sorry, Miss Nichols. My parents left for the Upper Peninsula yesterday to visit my grandparents and they won't be back until Monday."

Monday.

Kate closed her eyes. "It's very important that I get the order *today*. There has to be someone there who can help me out."

"I don't know what to do." Amber sounded as if she were on the verge of tears, which made Kate feel even worse. "It's the first time my parents put me in charge and I promised my dad he wouldn't have to worry about anything."

"It's okay." Kate wasn't sure how she found herself in the role of comforter when she was in dire need of some comfort herself! "I'll figure something out."

"You'll order from us again, won't you?"

"I'll talk to your parents when they get back." It was the only promise Kate could make.

The response was a faint sniffle. "All right."

"These kind of things happen," Kate heard

herself say. "It's all part of owning a business. It will work out."

Please let it work out.

At this late date, Kate wasn't sure where she would find what she needed, but she wasn't quite ready to release the mental image of her main entrée. Chicken, slow cooked to perfection, with a drizzle of her famous maple-syrup and cranberry glaze, nestled on a bed of wild rice pilaf. If worst came to worst, she would just have to revise the menu.

Abby wouldn't mind. Kate couldn't count the number of times over the past few months she had heard her friend say, "we aren't going to sweat the small stuff. The wedding is only a day, the marriage is forever."

It was good to know Abby felt that way but there was another opinion to consider and it wasn't Quinn's. Alex Let-Me-Hire-A-Real-Chef Porter would never let her forget it.

"Thank you so much for not yelling, Miss Nichols," Amber said. "And—"

Don't say it, Kate thought.

"Have a nice day!"

"Right." Kate hung up the phone with a

sigh, knowing Doug would be champing at the bit to get back on his route…

"Hey, Kate! Over here."

Or maybe not.

The truck driver was sitting at a booth near the window and he raised his fork in a mock salute. "The guy in the kitchen gave me this while I was waiting. Apple pie counts as a fruit, right?"

Knowing how busy she was getting ready for the wedding, Grady must have slipped in a few minutes early.

"Thanks, Grady!" she called.

"You're welcome."

Kate strangled on her next breath as Alex sauntered out of the kitchen.

Chapter Five

"What are you doing here?"

Alex showing up at her café at the crack of dawn was beginning to be a habit.

"I was out for a run and saw the lights on."

And it wasn't fair, Kate thought, that Alex looked better in black sweatpants and a plain cotton T-shirt than most men did in a tux. She tore her gaze away from his lean but solid frame and looked pointedly at the clock on the wall.

"The café isn't open yet."

"Doug let me in."

"Really." Kate wasted a scowl on the truck driver, who was so intent on tunneling his way through the massive piece of apple pie that he didn't even notice.

"He mentioned that you're having a little trouble with the order for the reception."

"No trouble," she denied sweetly.

"You got your chicken?" Doug had surfaced for air.

Not exactly, Kate wanted to say. But she couldn't with You Know Who standing right there.

Alex gave her a measuring look. "You'd tell me if there was anything wrong." It wasn't a question. "This is Abby's wedding and we want to make sure everything goes the way it should."

Translation: the way Alex Porter thought it should go.

"Really. Nothing is wrong." Nothing that fervent prayer and a few phone calls wouldn't fix, anyway.

Alex didn't look convinced. "Let me know if there's anything I can do. We *are* business partners."

"Not until Monday," Kate reminded him.

"You took on a partner?" Doug's head lifted like a hound on a scent trail.

"No!" Kate choked out. "I mean…Alex and I…our relationship has nothing to do with the café."

Seeing the gleam of interest in the man's eyes, she realized she shouldn't have used the word "relationship."

"It's not what you're thinking, Doug!"

"Don't worry." Doug winked at her. "Your secret is safe with me."

"There is no secret," Kate hissed. "We're helping out Abby and Quinn. That's all."

"I get it." Doug lumbered to his feet and gave Alex a good-natured jab in the side with his elbow. "You're a lucky guy. Kate's one in a million."

"Oh, I figured that out right away," Alex drawled.

"Don't encourage him," Kate said in a terse whisper.

Alex might frequently make the society pages of the Chicago newspapers—not that she'd looked—but it paled in comparison to how many people the unofficial grapevine of a small town could reach.

Doug's truck route zigzagged through the entire county. By sunset that evening, everyone he'd come into contact with would be speculating about Kate's relationship with Alex Porter.

Business relationship, she corrected herself.

The idea that she and Alex would—could—ever be anything else was...well, it was laughable.

Not only did Alex move in a social sphere far above that of mere mortals like herself, from what Kate had gleaned from her conversations with Abby, he also lived his life by a strict set of guidelines. The Grand Plan, Abby had ruefully called it during one of the times she'd lamented about her older brother.

Abby hadn't gone into detail, but it sounded as if everything on the list revolved around work.

That was something that Kate could understand. She devoted the majority of her time and energy to the café. But to her, it was less about serving food and more about serving *people*.

She and Alex Porter would never see eye-to-eye. His goal was to build an empire. Kate's was to build a life.

"Thanks for the pie." Doug reluctantly moved the plate aside, mopped his face with a napkin and pushed to his feet.

"You're welcome," Alex said.

Kate waited for him to follow Doug out the door. He took over the empty booth instead.

"I'll have coffee."

"I'm sorry." Kate tried to look as if she meant it. "The café isn't open yet."

Alex consulted a wristwatch that resembled the control panel of a jet. "It's six o'clock."

Kate glanced at *her* watch. The one shaped like a wedge of cheddar cheese that she'd won in a drawing during Dairy Days.

It *was* six o'clock.

"One coffee, coming up."

Kate no longer believed that Alex had come to Mirror Lake to check up on her.

He'd come to Mirror Lake to drive her crazy.

"You summoned?"

Alex glanced up and saw Quinn standing in the doorway of Abby's office.

"Very funny. You could always moonlight as a stand-up comedian if you don't make enough money in the security business. Or, here's a thought." He leaned back in the chair and considered his future-brother-in-law. "You could marry an heiress."

"Watch it or we won't invite you for Christmas." The tone was mild enough, but Alex didn't miss the flash of warning in Quinn's pewter-gray eyes.

"Who needs an invitation?" Alex hid a smile. No doubt about it, O'Halloran loved his sister. And he was protective of her. Alex had recently come to the conclusion that the guy might—just might—be good enough for Abby.

No point in telling Quinn that, though. Maybe on their twenty-fifth wedding anniversary. Or the fiftieth. As skeptical as Alex was about "happily-ever-after," there was something in the way Abby and Quinn looked at each other that told Alex they just might make it that far.

His sister had been floating around the place all day, smiling and humming as she took care of the last-minute wedding details. The last of the guests had checked out before lunch. Abby's decision to close the inn for the weekend had been a good one. Like ants at a picnic, a steady stream of people had been coming and going all morning, sprucing up the grounds and the stone chapel in the woods where the couple planned to exchange their vows.

"So, what's up?" Quinn wandered into Abby's office and folded in half to fit into one of dainty wicker chairs stationed by the windows overlooking the lake. "Abby said you wanted to talk to me."

"Since I'm sticking around for a few weeks, I wondered if you wanted me to keep an eye on things at O'Halloran Security, too."

Quinn laughed.

"Is that a 'yes' or a 'no'?"

"It's a no—thank you," Quinn added. "I appreciate the offer, but my employees are extremely capable and I've got Faye guarding the front office."

Capable. There was that word again. Alex was tempted to repeat the Porter family motto but decided it wouldn't do any good. Not only was Quinn *not* a Porter, but Alex had a strong suspicion he would agree with the version Abby had, in her words, *tweaked*.

The tough bodyguard-turned-security-specialist had a marshmallow center and Alex couldn't put all the blame on his sister. References to God—and not the ones typical to a former Marine—seemed to come as naturally to the guy as breathing.

"Just thought I'd offer." Alex shut down the computer program he'd been working on. Abby had given him full access to her records, so he'd spent the morning going through the inn's finances.

Surprisingly enough, even in a slow economy, Abby had been turning a decent profit. The cabins Quinn had renovated the previous summer were booked solid through the end of October. Once Abby decided to open up the rooms inside the main lodge to guests, Alex guessed those would fill up, as well.

"Believe me, you'll have plenty to do around here," Quinn said. "The locals love the fact that Abby reopened the inn and she encourages them to use the property."

Uh-huh. And, according to the records, she didn't charge them a thing.

His sister was asking to be taken advantage of. Alex had discovered that Church of the Pines, the one Quinn and Abby attended every Sunday, frequently scheduled events at the inn. Abby generously provided refreshments and, at times, invited visiting speakers to stay at the inn. Free of charge.

Alex made a mental note to talk to the pastor, Matthew Wilde, at some point over the next two weeks. Just so the guy knew that someone was looking out for Abby's best interests.

"There you are." Abby glided into the room, clutching the gaudiest shoes Alex had ever seen, a pair of white sneakers crusted with sparkling beads and pink sequins.

She smiled at Alex before zeroing in on her fiancé. "Could I talk to you for a minute, Quinn?"

"Sure."

"In the kitchen?" Abby bit her lower lip.

Alex recognized the gesture. Obviously Quinn did, too, because they both came to their feet at the same time.

"What's wrong?"

Abby smiled at Quinn. And frowned at Alex. "Nothing. There's always a few last-minute…glitches…to work out when it comes to weddings."

Alex looked at the shoes in her hand. "I see what you mean."

Abby chuckled. "I'm not talking about the shoes."

"Are you sure?"

"I'm sure. These are for Faye. She can't wear heels because of the arthritis in her feet, so Kate bedazzled her favorite pair of Keds."

"Bedazzled?" Alex looked at Quinn.

"I have no idea, but it sounds like something Kate would do," he said with a shrug.

Alex's eyes narrowed. "So does causing a glitch."

Abby cast Alex a meaningful look, silently reminding him of their conversation the night before. "Don't worry. Everything will be… everything *is* fine."

Where had he heard that before? Oh yes, in the Grapevine Café that morning.

"Does this have something to do with the chicken?" he demanded.

Abby's eyes went wide. "Kate told you?"

Actually, the tattooed, pie-eating truck driver had. He'd also told Alex—between bites—that the café's walk-in freezer had died and she'd lost a good portion of her inventory.

"I heard the order didn't come in."

Abby nodded. "Kate called about half an hour ago. The order was supposed to be on the truck, but she found out the supplier wrote down the wrong date. The chicken will arrive on time—a week from now."

"I hope that doesn't mean you want to postpone the wedding?" Quinn wrapped an arm around Abby's slender waist.

She smiled up at him. "Not a chance. It'll work out. Kate just wanted to let me know that she'll be a few minutes late for the rehearsal dinner. Thor is giving her grief again so she'll meet up with us at the restaurant."

"Her boyfriend's name is Thor?" Alex said before he could stop himself.

Abby grinned. "No. Her *car's* name is Thor. Kate's grandfather left her a Thunderbird when she was in high school, but the last few months it's been in the shop more than it's been on the road."

"That's because it attracts more attention than Charlie Pendleton's ice-cream truck,"

Quinn said. "Thor practically has his own following in this town. I think Happy takes his time fixing the car because people hang around the garage to admire it."

A car with a fan club and a mechanic named Happy. Eccentric didn't begin to describe this town, Alex thought.

"What about the reception dinner?" He pushed the conversation back on track.

"What about it?" Abby looked a little confused. Alex knew that too much stress could have that effect on a person.

"Is there going to *be* one?"

"Oh, if Kate says it's under control, believe me, it's under control."

Alex didn't believe it. Not for a minute. Kate was juggling too many plates. A crash was inevitable but he didn't want it to be on Abby's wedding day.

"It isn't like she has superpowers," he muttered.

Quinn and Abby glanced at each other.

"Well…" Abby drew out the word. "She and God make a pretty good team. If you ask Kate where she gets her energy, she'll tell you to look up Isaiah, chapter forty."

"I don't have time to look it up." Alex checked his watch. "We have to leave for the rehearsal dinner soon."

"Does Kate need a ride?" Quinn asked.

Abby shook her head. "No, she's got Penelope."

"Let me guess." Alex couldn't keep the sarcasm from leaking into his voice. "Penelope is a hot-air balloon."

"Now you're starting to get it," Quinn murmured.

"Penelope—" Abby shot her fiancé a quelling look "—is a bicycle."

"She's riding a bicycle. To the rehearsal dinner." Alex wanted to make sure he understood. Because of the size of the wedding, Abby and Quinn had opted for a small, informal gathering at a nearby supper club.

Alex had stopped in the day before and talked with the manager. With only a little persuasion and his signature on a check, the man had not only agreed to close the entire dining room while they were there, he'd promised to hire a local pianist to provide music during the meal.

But if Alex's memory served him correctly,

The Cedars had to be a good three or four miles west of town. For some reason, the thought of Kate pedaling that distance set his teeth on edge.

"I'll swing by the café and pick up Kate."

Abby's initial astonishment faded to caution. "I don't know if that's a good idea. She mentioned that she had a few loose ends to tie up before she could leave."

That's why it was a good idea. Alex didn't like loose ends. From what he knew about Kate, she probably viewed them as decorations.

Kate was officially late.

Clutching a handful of skirt with one hand, she tried to wrestle her bicycle out of the shed with the other. One of the tires had tangled with a metal rake and neither was cooperating with her efforts to set them free.

But then, not a whole lot of things had been cooperating.

Amber Jensen had called with an update around lunchtime. Another restaurant farther up the Chain of Lakes that had also placed an order for free-range chicken agreed to sell it to Kate. All she needed was someone to pick it up.

Unfortunately, Thor, her beloved but temperamental Thunderbird, was holding court in Happy's Garage until Monday, leaving Kate with no choice but to punch in Doug's number and offer a bribe. Retrieve the chicken and he had access to all the pie he could eat. For an entire month. Kate only hoped she wouldn't live to regret the offer.

Doug had come through. He'd dropped off the order only minutes before, giving Kate enough time to speed shower and change into a dress for the rehearsal dinner.

Abby had granted her full access to the inn's gourmet kitchen the next morning. With the ceremony taking place midafternoon, Kate would have plenty of time to prepare the meal and still be on hand to help Emma and Zoey with any last-minute details.

So, take that, Alex Porter...

"Acckk!"

The bike and the rake suddenly parted company and Kate stumbled backward, tripping over the friendly garden gnome one of her teenage waitresses had made in senior pottery class. She landed on her backside in the alley. Hard.

"Are you and Penelope having a disagreement?"

A tall, Alex Porter-shaped shadow momentarily blotted out the sun.

And just when her day had been looking a little brighter, too.

Kate winced. "How did you know her name?"

"Like someone once told me, it's a very small town."

"You did a background check, didn't you?"

"Don't be ridiculous. No one does a background check on a bicycle." Alex reached out a hand.

Choosing practicality over pride, Kate grabbed hold of it and let Alex draw her to her feet.

"Thanks." Even to her own ears, she sounded a little breathless. That had to have something to do with the fall and not because even the briefest touch of Alex's hand sent her pulse skipping like a rock over the surface of the water.

Kate shook the gravel off her skirt and spun

around several times, peering over her shoulder in a vain attempt to assess the damage. A bit dusty, but it could have been much worse...

"You look like a kitten chasing its tail."

Kate stopped midtwirl and parked her hands on her hips. "Why aren't you at the rehearsal dinner?" The question came out a little less grateful than it probably should have, given the fact that Alex *had* offered his assistance.

"I had to make a stop first. Abby mentioned you had a transportation problem."

It took Kate a moment to connect the dots. *She* was the stop.

The gesture would have been sweet...if it had been from anyone but Alex. He was a spy, not a knight in shining armor coming to her rescue.

Alex bent down to pick up her bicycle. The wicker basket attached to the front handlebars was askew and one of the plastic daisies had fallen off. Without asking permission, he wheeled the bicycle back into the storage shed behind the café and closed the door.

"Ready?"

To get into a car—alone—with Alex Porter? Not in this lifetime. But unless she wanted to hold up the rehearsal dinner any longer than she already had, Kate didn't see she had much choice in the matter.

"I parked in front," Alex said.

As Kate took a step forward, the heel of her shoe twisted and sank into the loose gravel.

Ordinarily she avoided wearing heels, but certain situations—like rehearsal dinners or times when she needed the advantage gained by adding a few inches to her diminutive height—called for them.

Glancing down, she saw that one of the straps had broken.

Drat. She'd have to switch them out for another pair.

"I'll be right back." Kate changed directions and began to hobble toward the café.

"What's wrong now?"

Kate didn't miss the emphasis on the last word. "My shoe broke."

"Does catastrophe follow you wherever you go?"

Kate whirled around and went up on her tiptoes, which put the top of her head level with Alex's chin. She looked him straight in the eye.

"Apparently so."

A split second of silence followed her statement.

Oh, no. Now she'd done it. Kate was never rude to people. *Never.* But Alex Porter brought out a snarky side that lay dormant most of the time.

She braced herself, not sure whether the comment warranted a lift of the eyebrow or a blistering set down or a...*smile.*

A real smile. A smile that stripped the breath from Kate's lungs and sent her heart flopping around in her chest like a freshly caught trout.

A smile that suddenly had Kate wondering if it wasn't just her sanity that was at risk for the next two weeks.

If she were smart, she'd better keep a close eye on her heart, as well.

Chapter Six

"You can't go in there. It's bad luck to see the bride before the wedding."

Alex scowled at the woman blocking his path. "I thought that was for the groom."

"It's whoever I say it is." Faye McAllister crossed her arms over her chest and didn't budge from her post in front of the bedroom door.

Alex struggled to keep a tight rein on his patience. When he'd climbed the stairs to Abby's third floor suite of rooms, he hadn't expected to find Quinn's receptionist standing guard like a Doberman in raspberry satin.

"I'm her brother."

"And I'm her bridesmaid," Faye retorted.

"I have to talk to her—" Alex bit off the rest of the sentence as the door opened and a familiar face, dominated by a pair of shamrock-green eyes, peeked out.

"I should have known."

Kate slipped into the hallway and pulled the door shut firmly behind her. Unless she planned to wear jean shorts and a bright yellow tank top for the ceremony, she hadn't taken time to change for the wedding yet.

"What's going on?"

Alex opened his mouth to speak, but Faye cut him off.

"He wants to talk to Abby."

Alex decided the woman might have been a little more intimidating had she not been wearing sequined tennis shoes.

Kate gave Faye's arm a reassuring pat. "It's all right. I can handle this one."

"All right, but holler if you need me." Faye swept past them, leaving a trail of Chanel N° 5 in her wake as she marched down the stairs.

Kate moved into position.

"You're replacing her as the bouncer?" Alex asked. "If this is what O'Halloran considers security, his business is in more trouble than I thought."

His gaze lingered for a moment on the tiny, heart-shaped charm dangling from the gold chain around Kate's ankle.

Her bare toes curled into the plush carpet and her cheeks turned the same shade of pearl pink as the nail polish she wore. "Faye is one of the reasons Quinn's business is successful."

"I'm surprised she doesn't scare away the customers," Alex muttered. "I couldn't sweet-talk my way past her."

"Is that what you were trying to do." Kate tipped her head. "On the other side of the door, it sounded like you were trying to pull rank."

"I need to talk to Abby."

"That's why Faye wouldn't let you in."

"That doesn't make any sense."

Kate simply looked at him until it did.

Alex blew out a sigh. "I wasn't going to talk Abby out of getting married."

"Really." Kate didn't sound too convinced, either.

"No." Alex wasn't used to having to explain himself but it was clear that Kate wasn't going to let him pass until he did. "I have… something for Abby. Something I need to give her before the ceremony."

"A prenup?"

"You are so…" Alex struggled to find the right word, something that he never struggled with.

"Insightful?" Kate supplied. "Wise beyond my years?"

Alex felt a smile coming on. And it was about as welcome as a case of the flu. Kate Nichols didn't seem to be the least bit intimidated by him. It left Alex feeling a little off balance.

Maybe he *was* coming down with the flu.

"It's not a prenup. It's a gift." Alex thrust his hand in the pocket of his tux and produced a small velvet jeweler's box as evidence. "You know that old poem."

"Poem?"

She was going to make him say it.

"Something old, something new…" Alex couldn't remember the rest so he opened the box. A delicate gold bracelet, adorned with a single pearl, lay across a pillow of pink satin.

"This is the something old. Dad gave it to our Mom and I thought Abby might want to wear it today."

Kate was staring. Not at the bracelet. At *him*.

"What?" Alex had opened the safe and looked through their mother's jewelry before he'd left for Mirror Lake. Every year on their anniversary, his father had bought their mother a piece of jewelry. There were more expensive pieces, but for some reason, Alex had kept coming back to this one. Now he wondered if he shouldn't have given Abby the diamond tennis bracelet instead.

When Kate didn't respond, he closed the box with a snap. "It's too plain."

A small freckled hand, unadorned with any jewelry at all, closed over the box before he could put it away.

"No! It's beautiful," Kate contradicted. "Abby will love it."

There was a slight catch in her voice. And to Alex's absolute amazement, her eyes had misted over.

"Are you *crying?*"

Kate's chin lifted in a gesture he was beginning to recognize. "I always cry at weddings."

Alex didn't point out the obvious. That the wedding hadn't even started yet.

"That's very sentimental." He couldn't quite prevent the urge to point *that* out.

"It's also perfectly acceptable," Kate shot back. "As long as they're happy tears."

Happy tears?

"Isn't that a contradiction?"

"Only if you've never experienced it." Kate rapped on the door and opened it a crack. "Abby? There's someone here to see you."

It took Alex a moment to realize that she'd stepped to the side.

"Tell Abby I'll be back in a few minutes." Kate ducked past him.

"Kate?"

She paused at the top of the stairs and looked back, a question in her eyes.

Alex unleashed a slow smile. "The prenup is in my other pocket."

As soon as the door closed behind him, Kate collapsed against the stair rail and closed her eyes.

What was more disturbing than Alex Porter in a tuxedo?

A crack in Alex Porter's Armani armor, revealing a side to the man that Kate wouldn't have thought existed, that's what.

Kate would have guessed that Alex would follow tradition by giving Abby something over the top. Say, a tiara. Or a diamond bracelet from Tiffany's. He had accused her of being overly sentimental and yet he'd chosen a modest piece of jewelry for Abby because it had a special connection to their mother.

And the glimmer of uncertainty in his eyes when he'd asked if the bracelet was too plain made him seem more…human.

Kate didn't want him to be human.

It was much easier to keep her distance when he played the part of the stuffy, condescending executive, not the *caring* older brother who wanted to give Abby a reminder of the parents who couldn't be there on her wedding day.

"There you are, Kate!" Esther Redstone spotted her at the top of the stairs. "How is our bride-to-be?"

"Beautiful," Kate said promptly.

No wedding-day jitters for Abby. Her friend was practically glowing with anticipation.

There was no doubt in Kate's mind that God had brought the couple together. She was thrilled for her friend, but she couldn't but feel a tiny—very tiny—pinch of envy.

In high school, Kate had promised God that she would wait for the right man—the one that *He* had chosen for her. She just hadn't expected it to take so long.

Anytime, Lord. Really.

"I peeked in the kitchen a few minutes ago. Everything looks wonderful. And the cake!" Esther chuckled. "Very creative."

"Abby didn't want a traditional wedding cake. She told me to use my imagination." The result being four dozen miniature cakes with chocolate mousse centers and slathered in butter-cream frosting, decorated to look like campfire s'mores. Abby's favorite dessert.

"I better check to make sure Cody is ready." Esther's blue eyes twinkled. "Not that I don't trust my husband to get the boy ready, but

I've been straightening that man's tie for over forty years."

"I appreciate that. Cody looked a little nervous during the rehearsal."

Although that could have been Alex's fault. Kate had seen his surprise when Abby introduced him to Cody Lang and Daniel Redstone the night before. Alex hadn't said anything, but it was clear he hadn't expected Quinn to choose the adolescent boy he mentored and a semi-retired carpenter as his groomsmen.

Esther cleared her throat. "I can't wait to see your dress, my dear. Faye said it's lovely."

"Dress?" Kate blinked, feigning ignorance. "No one said anything about a dress."

But maybe that explained why Alex had been staring at her bare feet. Maybe he assumed she would show up at the wedding in cut-off shorts and a tank top.

But Esther, who had known Kate since she was a baby, simply laughed as she bustled away. "I'll see you at the ceremony."

The main lodge was bustling with activity when Kate made her way downstairs. Although the wedding wasn't until three o'clock, some of the guests, like Esther, had arrived early to help with preparations.

Through the glass doors leading to the deck, Kate spotted her two friends, Emma Sutton and Zoey Decker, sitting at a wicker table, putting together the bridal bouquet from the wildflowers she'd picked on her way to the inn that morning.

As temperamental as northern Wisconsin weather could be—even in early August— it was a perfect day. Both the lake and the sky had dressed in blue for the occasion and sunlight beaded the water, matching Abby's dress sparkle for sparkle.

"How is Abby holding up?" Emma wrapped an ivory velvet ribbon around a sprig of pink heirloom rosebuds.

"Great." Kate picked up a daisy and rolled the stem between her fingers. "I left her with Alex a few minutes ago."

Emma's smoke-blue eyes widened. "On purpose?"

"He promised he wasn't going to talk her out of getting married."

The doubtful look Emma and Zoey exchanged made Kate glad she hadn't mentioned Alex's teasing comment about the prenup.

Because he *had* been teasing. Hadn't he?

"I heard that you and Alex are going to be running the inn while Abby and Quinn are on their honeymoon," Emma ventured.

"I'm only going to be here a few hours a day. Our paths shouldn't cross that often. Alex will be working in the office. I'll be in the kitchen—"

"Like Cinderella," Zoey interrupted with a grin.

Kate made a face. Until Zoey had made Mirror Lake her permanent home recently, she'd played the lead in a modern version of the popular fairy tale at a dinner theatre in the Wisconsin Dells. Zoey might have found her "happily ever after" with Matthew Wilde, one of Kate's close friends and the pastor of the church she attended; but there was no way she would let *her* friend cast her in that role.

Especially with Alex Porter.

Even if he looked spectacular in a tuxedo. And had a smile that appeared out of nowhere and streaked through her like summer lightning.

Kate was still experiencing the aftershock of that smile.

She hadn't expected to discover a razor-sharp sense of humor lurking below his implacable surface.

She hadn't expected him to make her laugh. Or to laugh at himself.

Two qualities Kate had always dreamed of in a man.

She shoved the thought aside.

Sense of humor or not, a man like Alex Porter didn't belong in Mirror Lake.

And he sure didn't belong in her dreams.

"So?" Abby took a slow spin in front of the full-length mirror and sent yards of ivory satin belling out from her trim waist. "What do you think?"

Alex's throat tightened. "I think that Mom and Dad would be very proud of you."

Abby's smile faded. She launched herself into his arms and Alex rocked her back and forth, the same way he had the night they'd received the news about their parents.

"I wish they were here," she whispered against his shoulder.

"So do I." Because then he would be the doting older brother, watching from the sidelines, not the one walking Abby down the aisle. Giving her away. "I brought you something."

"Alex." Abby's eyes rounded when she saw the jewelry box. "I wasn't expecting a gift."

"Just following tradition."

"Tradition?"

"Don't make me say it again." Alex closed his eyes, as if in pain. "Although some people might argue that I qualify as the 'something old.'"

"Oh, *that* tradition." Abby's laughter died as she opened the lid. Tentatively, she reached out and touched the pearl. "This was Mom's favorite piece of jewelry."

"I didn't know that."

Abby nodded. "It was the first gift he bought for her. She told me that Dad had to wash dishes every night for a month in order to pay for it."

Alex had never heard the story, but he didn't doubt it was true. At sixteen, their parents had met while working at a resort in Lake Geneva for the summer. By the end of August, they had set two goals. To marry after they graduated from high school and to eventually own their own hotel.

They'd succeeded at both.

To honor their memory, Alex had continued the family legacy.

He carefully clasped the delicate bracelet around Abby's wrist and she hugged him again. "You don't know how much this means to me." Alex heard the distinct sound of a sniffle. "I'm sorry. I know you hate emotional f-females."

"It's perfectly acceptable to cry on your wedding day as long as they're...happy tears."

Abby took a step back and peered up at him. "Okay, who are you and what have you done with my brother?"

"Maybe it's all this fresh air and sunshine. I'm not used to it."

"You aren't used to any of this." Abby smiled. "I told you that Mirror Lake is special. It changes a person. It makes you long for things you never even knew you wanted."

"I have everything I want."

Abby straightened his tie. "But you don't have everything you *need*."

"Is there a difference?"

"Yes—"

A knock at the door spared him another one of Abby's lectures.

"Come in," she called out.

The door swung open, revealing Jake Sutton on the other side. His gaze flickered from Abby's tear-stained face to Alex.

"Is everything all right?" The question was directed at Abby, but the slight frown that settled between his brows was definitely meant for Alex.

Kate had probably sent the guy up to check on Abby. But the local chief of police? Not exactly subtle.

Alex realized he was smiling. Again.

"Everything is fine." Abby dabbed at her eyes with a tissue. "We were just talking about our parents."

Understanding dawned in Jake's eyes and he nodded. "I'm supposed to tell you that everyone left for the chapel a few minutes ago. Are you ready?"

Tears still glimmered in Abby's eyes but her smile was radiant. "Yes."

Alex decided it was probably a good thing the police chief didn't ask him if *he* was ready.

Chapter Seven

"Kate, come outside. Abby is about to throw the wedding bouquet!"

Kate was already shaking her head. "No way."

"But you're the maid of honor!" Haylie Owens and Morgan Peterson, two girls from the church youth group who had been helping in the kitchen, continued to advance on her.

"At the moment, I'm the caterer." Kate skirted around the island and patted the apron that covered her dress. "See?"

"There are only six women. I counted. You've got a really good chance," Morgan said earnestly.

A really good chance of being the first

maid of honor ever to spontaneously combust from acute embarrassment!

"No one will miss me—"

"Kate Nichols." The bride herself swished into the kitchen. "Where have you been? Everyone is waiting for you!"

"Go ahead without me, Abby. It's almost time to serve the cake."

"We can put it on the trays," Haylie offered.

"Thanks," Kate said through gritted teeth. "But—"

"No more excuses." Abby latched onto Kate's arm and tugged her through the doorway. "Stand a little to the left of the hydrangea bush," she whispered.

"You're *rigging* the bouquet toss?" Kate tried to dig in her heels…only she wasn't wearing heels. And ballet flats, she quickly discovered, provided no traction whatsoever.

Abby didn't look the least bit guilty. "You still have to catch it."

"Abby, I don't—" Kate balked when she spotted Alex near the gazebo.

"What's the matter?" Abby gave her a gentle push toward the small cluster of single women, most of them friends from church. "This will be fun. You love fun, Kate."

She did love fun. When she wasn't being *scrutinized*.

All afternoon and into the evening, Kate had felt as if she were under a microscope—as if Alex were waiting for her to make a mistake. Even though everyone had raved about the food, he hadn't said a word, good or bad.

Come to think of it, he hadn't said much at all. Nor had he mingled with the guests.

Was she the only one who noticed how Alex held himself apart? How he seemed to watch the world rather than participate in it?

Abby had said that Alex had lost his faith in people when she was abducted; and his faith in God when their parents died.

Kate had experienced her share of pain. Losing her mother to breast cancer when she was a senior in high school had left a terrible void in Kate's life. But it was her faith in God, and the love and compassion of a small town, that had gotten her through those first difficult months and beyond.

Alex had been there for Abby, but had anyone been there for him?

Lord, You always have a purpose. There must be a reason why You brought Alex here...show him that You're real and that You love him.

For the first time, Kate found herself praying for the man himself, rather than an extra measure of patience to deal with him!

"No amount of dragging your feet or muttering will get you out of this," Abby said cheerfully.

"I wasn't muttering." Kate couldn't deny the "dragging her feet" part. "I was praying." She decided not to mention just whose name she had brought to the Lord's attention.

"Praying I understand. But keep your eyes open or you might miss the bouquet."

"You can do it, Kate!" Zoey and Emma waved as Abby towed her past the buffet table.

It wasn't fair that her closest friends were exempt from the tradition because of the diamond rings on their fingers. Kate crossed her eyes before she was sucked into a vortex of tulle and satin.

* * *

Alex watched his sister tug a laughing Kate toward the flock of women standing near the butterfly garden.

Who was he kidding? He'd been watching Kate for most of the day.

The transformation had been startling.

Gone were the faded denim shorts and tank top. Triple strands of thin gold metal, studded with tiny faux diamonds, were threaded through her hair like a crown and glinted like dewdrops in the cap of auburn curls. A strapless dress hugged Kate's slender curves, the filmy skirt a watercolor print of soft pinks, blues and greens that swept the tops of pale green ballet flats.

At the chapel, she had played the part of the attentive maid of honor, dispensing smiles and tissues to whoever needed them. Between the ceremony and the reception, she led the guests into the garden with the skill of a general commanding his troops and then gamely posed for the photographer. The next time Alex saw Kate, she was emerging from the kitchen in a white apron, helping the teenagers set up the buffet table.

She'd made sure the lights twinkled, the music didn't overpower the conversation and that the food was served piping hot.

The food.

Alex had taken a brief reconnaissance mission to the kitchen early in the day to see what Kate had done with the elusive order of chicken. When he lifted the lid on the counter-top roaster, the aroma alone made his stomach roll over and beg.

There were plump pieces of chicken, threaded on long wooden skewers, cooked in a light sauce, the distinct tang of cranberries complimented by a mysterious sweetness. Simple. Delicious. And something one of his chefs would have served with pride.

If Kate had the ability to create something like that, why was the café's menu crowded with predictable but unimaginative offerings like hamburgers and meat loaf with mashed potatoes?

Alex couldn't figure it out.

He couldn't figure *her* out.

A sudden commotion snagged Alex's attention.

Right before Kate joined the other women,

she grabbed Faye McAllister's hand. Faye resisted for a moment, her cheeks turning as pink as the Keds on her feet, before letting herself be pulled into the circle.

"Everyone gather around," a gray-haired woman holding a pink cane bellowed. "The bride is going to toss the bouquet now!"

Abby looked at Kate, smiled and jerked her chin to the right. As soon as her back was turned, Kate inched to the left.

"Three. Two. One…"

The guests let out a loud cheer as Abby released the bouquet in a high arch, ribbons streaming like the tail of comet.

All the women leaped toward the bouquet as if they'd been launched out of a catapult.

Kate lifted her arms and the bouquet sailed right between them. She managed to grab hold of one of the streamers…and it unraveled as it continued on its course.

Straight toward Alex—who had a split second to decide if he wanted to catch the bouquet or wear it.

He caught it.

A chorus of cheers erupted from the onlookers.

"Look! A guy caught it!" A teenage girl pointed at him.

"He caught Kate, too!" another one giggled.

Alex realized that he was holding on to the bouquet…and Kate was still holding on to the streamer.

"Someone get a ladder for Kate next time," a man standing next to Alex chuckled.

"Does this mean they're both going to get married?"

"Does this mean they're going to marry each other?"

They were drawing a larger crowd than the wedding cake, all pressing for a closer look. Pressing him and Kate together.

"Why did you catch it?" Kate grumbled under her breath.

"Because it went over your head," Alex reminded her in a low voice. "Why didn't *you* let go?"

The photographer waded through the crowd with his camera. "Since both of you caught it, you can pose for Abby's photo album together."

"You know what they say." Kate dropped

the streamer as if it were a fuse someone had just lit. "Possession is nine tenths of the law!"

She aimed a sunny smile at Alex before she danced away.

"Don't forget to say cheese!"

Two hours later, the guests had left and the taillights of Quinn's truck disappeared around a corner. The last vehicle parked in the driveway was a black Thunderbird.

Alex tracked Kate to the kitchen. A dish-towel was knotted around her trim waist, the ballet slippers at her feet by the sink.

She was humming one of the songs that Zoey Decker had sung during the ceremony. Something about love and commitment and a whole lot of other things Alex had stopped believing in about the same time he stopped believing in Santa Claus and the Tooth Fairy.

Kate did a little two-step to the side as she reached for another dish.

"Go home, Kate."

The slender shoulders tensed. Relaxed. She turned to face him, iridescent bubbles cling-ing to both hands. "I think that sounded like an order."

"You think?" Alex leaned a shoulder against the doorjamb. "Then I must have not done it right."

A hint of a smile touched Kate's lips. How could she look as fresh as one of the daisies in Abby's bouquet after being on her feet since five o'clock?

"I'm almost finished."

"Go home," he repeated softly. "I've got a cleanup crew coming in tomorrow."

"I should remind you, that right now you're in the kitchen, which is *my* jurisdiction."

"Not quite." Alex looked down at the strip of wood that divided the ceramic tile from the hardwood flooring in the hallway.

Kate's eyes narrowed as she thought about that. Alex found himself looking forward to her response.

"Technically, *you* can't…" She ruined the effect by stifling a yawn. "Give me orders until Monday."

"Consider this a practice round."

"I thought you had already perfected the art of telling people what to do."

So had Alex.

But something told him that Kate wasn't

"people." No doubt about it. They were going to drive each other crazy for the next two weeks.

But even more crazy?

Alex found himself looking forward to it.

Chapter Eight

Humming along with the classical music she'd put on, Kate snapped open a red-and-white checkered cloth and let it drift over the top of the kitchen table in her apartment.

Once that was in place, she skipped back to the stove, lifted the lid on the enormous cast-iron kettle and gave the marinara sauce another stir. Kate's nose twitched appreciatively as the scent of tomatoes, garlic and fresh herbs perfumed the air.

Almost ready.

Dumping a batch of homemade linguini into a pan of boiling water, Kate set the timer and then raided the cabinets for her eclectic blend of china plates.

Most people in their right mind would be taking a nap the day after catering a wedding reception, not preparing another meal. But Kate wasn't most people. And others, oh, like the man who'd all but *ordered* her to go home and get some sleep after said reception, might argue that she wasn't in her right mind.

A foreshadowing of things to come.

Fortunately, Kate didn't have to report to the inn until Monday morning. The first guests, a Mr. and Mrs. Charlie Gibson, wouldn't be checking in until later in the afternoon, which gave her time to plan and prepare the breakfast menu. Something that Alex had no control over.

Kate smiled as she took a loaf of bread out of the oven.

Something brushed against her leg and she glanced down. "No, this isn't for you," she told the enormous rust-colored tabby curled around her ankle. "I'm sure Mr. Lundy will bring you a nice can of tuna."

Her friend loved animals, but because pets weren't allowed in the retirement home where he lived, Mr. Lundy had a tendency to spoil her two cats rotten.

Kate heard a rap on the door and smiled. He was also the first to arrive.

She opened the door. "Right on time…"

"You don't have a security system. Or a lock on your door."

Kate winced as Alex strode past her.

Ambushed again.

"I'll get on that." As soon as possible.

"You don't answer your phone, either." Alex stopped in the middle of the room, which suddenly seemed a lot smaller than it had ten seconds ago. "I didn't realize you lived above the café."

And yet he'd found out. Kind of disturbing. But what Kate found even more disturbing was the way her pulse started jumping like a hyperactive terrier whenever Alex was nearby.

"I grew up in a house a few blocks from Main Street, but Dad sold it when he relocated to Arizona, so I moved into the apartment. It's very convenient. I like it." *And you're rambling, Kate.*

"Convenient." Alex nodded. Something in his expression told her that particular description was the only one that fit.

Kate's gaze swept the room. She tried to see the apartment through his eyes. The furniture had seen better days, so she had hidden the outdated fabric under white canvas slipcovers and colorful pillows. Watercolors by local artists strategically covered the holes in walls that she'd painted a delicious shade of yellow.

Kate loved having a space to call her own. It just happened to be a very small one.

Face it, Kate. Your entire apartment would probably fit in the man's walk-in closet.

Alex's gaze snagged on the stack of stoneware plates that Kate had stationed at the end of the table. "You're expecting company?"

"I think so."

The eyebrow rose. "You *think* so?"

How to explain this in a way that Alex would understand?

Kate decided there wasn't one. "Every Sunday after church I make dinner for… people."

Alex shifted his attention to the enormous kettle of sauce bubbling away on the stove. "How many people?"

"Oh, anywhere from two to…twelve." The

week before, she'd had eighteen, but that had been a record number.

"Twelve?" he repeated.

"Give or take a few."

At the beginning of the summer, Kate had designated Sunday afternoons as her official "traveling day" even though she never ventured farther than the front door. After church, she chose a meal from the international cookbook her dad had given her the Christmas before.

The trouble was, Kate always made way too much food for one person. So she'd started to pray that God would bring to mind a person, or people, to share it with. But something unexpected had happened along the way. Her friends and neighbors heard about it and had started to simply show up at the door—without an invitation.

The first time she'd ended up with more people than she had chairs to sit in, Kate had been a bit flustered. But everyone had such a good time, laughing through the meal and lingering over dessert that now she left the guest list in the Lord's hands. Kate figured that God would bring the right people to her door and He did.

Most of the time.

"Let me get this straight. You have people coming over but you don't know how many."

"Right."

"How many did you invite?"

"I didn't exactly *invite* anyone." The timer went off and Kate dashed to the stove. "Excuse me."

"Kate?"

"Mmm?" Where had she put the colander?

"I'm being attacked."

She glanced over her shoulder and saw Alex keeping a wary eye on the two cats circling his feet. "The orange one is Lucy, the white one is Ethel, and they aren't attacking you. They love people."

"Uh-huh." Judging from Alex's tone, the feeling wasn't mutual.

"Don't you have any pets? A dog or a cat? Horses? Shark tank?"

Oops. Sorry, Lord. I just can't seem to help myself.

"No." A smile pulled at the corners of

Alex's lips and Kate felt a responding tug on her heart.

"I get it. Animals aren't part of The Grand Plan."

"What grand plan?" The smile disappeared and his voice dropped ten degrees.

Um, the grand plan she shouldn't have mentioned?

"Everyone has…goals, right? I want to cook my way around the world—I'm going to Italy today, by the way—and I want to knit something bigger than a potholder." And she was rambling again. "But I'm sure you didn't come over to listen to me go on and on." Kate paused, sucked in a breath and rushed on, "Why did you come over, by the way?"

"I found a note on Abby's desk that I can't decipher," he said abruptly. "I thought you might be able to tell me what it means."

Business. Of course that was the reason he'd sought her out. The man probably had no clue how to relax on a beautiful Sunday afternoon.

"Sure. I'll take a look." Anything to divert his attention from her knowledge of the master plan.

Alex dug a piece of paper out of the front pocket of his jeans and gave it to her.

Kate peered at the handwriting. "You can't decipher it because Quinn writes in his own personal brand of hieroglyphics. It looks like he scheduled a picnic for the mentoring ministry at church. Abby usually provides the food but I'll call Matt tomorrow and find out for sure."

Alex frowned. "Abby didn't mention a picnic."

"She probably forgot in all the pre-wedding whirl." Kate turned the paper sideways. "If I'm reading it right, the date is set for this coming Saturday. That makes sense, because guests check out of the inn by noon and that frees up the grounds for the kids."

"Kids?"

"Boys," she amended. And then, hoping to see him sweat, added, "Fifteen of them."

"Do I have to do anything?"

Since Alex's tone matched the one she'd heard when he was glowering down at her cats, Kate could only deduce that he wasn't fond of children, either.

"The mentors plan all the activities." She

drained the pasta and emptied it into a color-ful ceramic bowl. When she turned around again, Alex was examining the row of por-celain trinket boxes lined up on the window sill.

He picked up her favorite, a bird's nest.

"Open it."

Alex gave her a look.

Good grief.

"It's not a booby trap." Kate crossed the room, plucked it out of his hand and lifted the lid.

Alex stared down at the tiny blue egg inside. "What do you do with it?"

Do with it? No one had ever asked Kate that before.

"It's a trinket box. My grandma gave me the first one on my eighth birthday." She pointed to a carousel horse. "I was so ex-cited when I found the little gold key inside. It was like getting two gifts. She gave one to me every year after that.

"After she passed away, I kept collecting them. I try to match them to a memory. See this lighthouse? I bought that one in Door County."

"But once you open it, then what?" he persisted. "You already know what's inside."

"That's true." Kate smiled. "But then I get to see someone else's face when *they* open it."

Was she for real?

Alex set the box down on the windowsill. Along with the bird's nest and the carousel horse, there was a miniature English cottage, a sand castle and a sailboat.

"You can open the rest of them if you want to."

"That's all right." Alex caught a fleeting look of disappointment on Kate's face before she turned away, and he was tempted to take back the words.

But he hadn't stopped by to socialize.

"I'm surprised you feel up to having company today," he said abruptly. "You stayed at the inn until almost midnight."

Until he'd all but kicked her out.

Alex hadn't let himself feel guilty about telling her to go home. Even the Energizer Bunny needed to recharge its batteries once in awhile.

Kate shrugged. "I have to eat. It doesn't take much effort to stretch out the meal to include a few more."

Stretch out the meal? From the number of plates stacked on the table, it looked as if she were expecting an army.

The aroma of fresh-baked bread reminded Alex that he hadn't eaten since breakfast. Abby had stocked the kitchen before she left, but he'd skipped lunch and gone for a short run.

The inn had been quiet upon his return. Too quiet. He'd spent a few hours in the office, organizing things to suit his own system before discovering the note about the mentoring ministry picnic.

That's when he'd decided to pay Kate a visit.

Alex glanced down at the wool area rug that didn't quite cover the scuffed hardwood floor.

The café couldn't be doing very well if all she could afford was the cramped apartment on the floor above it. Two open bookcases formed a divider between the kitchen and the living room.

No wonder Abby had offered her the opportunity to cater the reception dinner. As a friend of Kate's, she would know if the business was struggling.

"I didn't see a bill. Did Abby pay you already?"

Kate tipped her head. "Pay me for what?"

"For the reception dinner."

The constellation of freckles on Kate's nose seemed to deepen in color.

"Abby doesn't owe me anything." She rattled a drawer open and began to remove the forks. And knives.

"I'll write a check, then. Just tell me what she owes."

"No one owes me anything." Kate wouldn't look at him now. "Providing the food was my *gift* to Quinn and Abby."

She'd donated the food. And her time.

Before Alex could process all the ramifications of that unexpected information, there was a knock at the door.

"Excuse me." Kate whisked past him to greet her visitor, her tone more enthusiastic than the one Alex had heard when she'd greeted *him*. "You don't have to knock, Mr. Lundy. You're family."

A gray-haired man shuffled in, a leather case clutched under one arm and a checkered fedora cradled in the other. "I'm sorry I'm a few minutes late, my dear. Every week it seems to take me longer to climb those stairs."

Alex instantly recognized him as the customer who had gone behind the counter to make a milkshake.

Kate tucked her arm through his and led him inside. "I love the zinnia. Very dashing," she added in a whisper.

Mr. Lundy looked down at the flower tucked in the top buttonhole of his seersucker jacket and beamed. "Marsha loves to garden, you know. She won a blue ribbon at the county fair every year."

"I remember."

"Orange is her favorite color…" He fingered the fragile petals and a faraway look came into his eyes. "But Marsha didn't plant a garden this year, did she?"

"Not this summer, no," Kate said softly.

"Alex, this is Mr. Arthur Lundy. Mr. Lundy, Alex Porter."

"It's nice to meet you, sir." Alex took the man's trembling hand in a firm but careful grip.

Faded blue eyes studied him. "I've told Kate time and time again to find herself a beau. I'm glad she finally took my advice."

Kate's cheeks turned a fascinating shade of pink. "Alex isn't my *beau,* Mr. Lundy. He's—"

"Her boss," Alex said helpfully.

Kate skewered him with a look. "Abby's brother, actually."

"*And* her boss."

"Temporary boss," Kate muttered.

"Marsha and I worked together for years." Arthur chuckled as he shuffled over to the sofa and set the case down on the coffee table. "Didn't always agree, but that only made life more interesting. If you argue, then you get to make up."

Now Alex felt warm as a sudden image of "making up" with Kate pushed its way in.

Arthur fumbled with the clasp on the case

and Alex intervened, grateful for the distraction. "Let me help you with that, Mr. Lundy."

He opened the lid. Nestled against a background of jet-black satin was a chessboard inlaid with mother-of-pearl and a set of hand-carved pieces. "This is beautiful craftsmanship. I've never seen anything like it."

"You play?"

"My father taught me when I was seven."

"Ah!" The man's eyes brightened. "A worthy opponent."

"What do you mean? I'm a worthy opponent!" Kate protested.

"Of course you are." Arthur turned back to him. "Everyone at Maplewood prefers checkers or pinochle, so I've been teaching Kate how to play. She tends to be very…bold…in her moves."

"Bold is good," Kate said under her breath.

Arthur began setting up a row of pawns. "Not very patient, though," he mused. "Kate doesn't *move* her pieces as much as she, what's the word I'm looking for…"

"Hurtles them around the board?" Alex guessed.

"Yes, yes! It's like she's shooting marbles

instead of playing chess." Arthur chuckled. "You know our Kate well."

She wasn't his Kate and he didn't know her at all.

But you want to.

The thought hit Alex like a sucker punch. He was still gasping for air when Kate flounced away.

"I'll let you two continue to talk about me while I check on dinner," she tossed over her shoulder.

"Marsha was a redhead like Kate," Arthur whispered. "That made life interesting, too."

Chapter Nine

Kate resisted the urge to clamp her hands over her ears.

Arthur Lundy had been like an adopted grandfather to her over the years, which meant he was anxious to see her "settle down" with the man of her dreams.

If only he knew that Alex had the starring role in some of her most recent nightmares. In the most recent one, she'd set fire to a dessert tray and it wasn't even crème brûlée!

"Sit down." Arthur sat back and gestured toward a chair. "I've been looking forward to this all day."

Out of the corner of her eye, Kate saw Alex hesitate. He would be anxious to leave now that he'd gotten the answer he had come for.

"I'm sorry—" Alex stopped.

Kate half turned, wondering why he hadn't finished the sentence.

Arthur's smile had faded, the white knight clutched in his hand as he stared at the board in confusion.

"Mr. Lundy?" Alex prompted softly.

"I can't…" Arthur blinked several times, as if he had been in the darkness and was now trying to adjust to the light.

Kate's heart wrenched. A few months after his wife's death, Mr. Lundy had begun to manifest the early signs of Alzheimer's. Kate understood the reason behind the occasional lapses, but Alex didn't—and he wasn't a man known for his patience.

She took a step forward, ready to intervene, but Alex was already pulling up a folding chair. He sat down, picked up the black knight and carefully and deliberately set it in place.

After a heartbeat of silence, Arthur mirrored the move and set his horse down on the opposite side of the board. "Very good. Very good," he murmured.

Alex leaned back. "I believe it's your move, Mr. Lundy."

* * *

Kate wanted to throw her arms around Alex and hug him.

That was crazy, given the fact that he wasn't exactly huggable…for an instant, Kate imagined herself trapped in the circle of his arms.

And groaned.

Both heads swung in her direction.

"Something wrong, Kate?" Arthur called.

"Nothing." *Everything.*

What was this? Sleep deprivation? Post-wedding stress syndrome? She couldn't be *attracted* to Alex.

He was the equivalent of a human ice sculpture. Every feature incredibly, startlingly perfect. But emotionless. Cold.

Except, a still, small voice inside reminded her, for the fact that Alex had gently restored an elderly man's dignity. The reason she had been tempted to hug him in the first place. And when he smiled…

She closed a drawer with a little more force than was necessary.

Get a grip, Kate.

Putting all thoughts of Alex—and his

arms—on lockdown, Kate removed the antipasto platter from the refrigerator.

"I smell pasta!" The door opened and Jeremy Sutton skidded toward her across the hardwood floor.

"Hi, Jeremy." Kate leaned down to hug the boy, who, at twelve, was still young enough to tolerate that kind of affection from the adults in his life. "You have a very good nose."

Jake and Emma stopped just inside the door and were staring at Alex, the expression on their faces similar to the one Kate had seen when she proudly showed off the feathered lampshade she had purchased at an estate sale. A sort of "what are you going to do with it" look.

When Emma glanced her way, Kate's shoulders lifted in a "I have no idea" shrug.

Jake broke the ice. He took a few steps forward and extended his hand. "Good to see you again, Alex."

Alex half rose to his feet and gripped the police chief's hand. "Sutton." His gaze shifted to the slender woman standing beside Jake. "Emma."

"Hello," Emma murmured.

Jeremy snitched a piece of cheese from a tray on the counter. "Me and Cody are going to build a tree house. We're drawing up the plans today."

As if on cue, the door opened again and Cody Lang slipped into the apartment like a shadow.

He dipped his head, finding the floor easier to talk to than an actual person. "Hey, Miss Nichols."

"Hello, Cody." Kate greeted him with a smile, knowing better than to hug the teenager the way she had hugged Jeremy Sutton. Abby and Quinn had worked hard over the past year to bring Cody out of his shell. He was sweet and hardworking, but a difficult home life had inflicted wounds that were slow to heal. "You and Jeremy know where the soda is. Help yourselves."

Another tap on the door. Kate took a silent tally and pulled out a few more plates.

"I can't believe you felt like cooking today, but we could smell the garlic two blocks away..." Zoey swept into the apartment, the rest of the sentence dying a natural death as she spotted the two men playing chess. "Alex."

It came out sounding like a question rather than a statement.

"Kate's beau," Arthur said without looking up.

"Boss," Kate corrected. Then, seeing the satisfied look on Alex's face, added, *"Temporary."*

Zoey flashed a warm smile. "Matt and I were hoping Kate would invite you over for dinner. The inn must seem pretty quiet now that the wedding is over and Abby and Quinn are gone."

She hadn't invited Alex, and he *prefers* quiet, Kate wanted to howl. What he *didn't* like were animals and children. And small towns. That happened to be three of her favorite things.

"It is," Alex admitted, shocking Kate to the tips of her pink toenails. "Abby is supposed to call when they get into London tonight."

Zoey enveloped Kate in a quick hug. "Matt is on his way. He and Harold Davis met after the service to go over a few details for the mentoring picnic next Saturday."

"It's going to be awesome." Jeremy's eyes sparkled. "Dad is going to ask Mr. McGuire to teach us about survival camping."

"Devlin McGuire?" Kate looked to Jake for confirmation.

"I know he doesn't normally talk to groups, but Harold thought he might make an exception for the mentoring ministry," Jake said. "I'm still waiting for him to get back to me."

Kate had her doubts that he would. The wildlife photographer had a reputation for being a bit of a recluse. On the rare occasions he came into the café, Dev was polite but didn't mingle with the locals.

Like someone else she knew.

Alex's head—and his eyebrow—lifted as the door opened again. At least now he knew she hadn't been exaggerating about the number of guests.

"We're here and we're hungry!" Liz Decker, Zoey's grandmother, and her friend Delia Peake trudged in, weighted down with the oversize canvas bags that held their knitting.

"That's good, because I've got plenty of food." Kate had tripled the recipe and had a backup salad in case of an emergency.

"Where are we going today, Kate?" Delia wanted to know.

Kate glanced at Alex. When she'd told him that she was having people over for dinner, she had left out the part about what kind of dinner it was. On purpose.

"Italy," she murmured.

"What did you say?" Delia leaned forward. "New Delhi?"

"Italy," Kate repeated, a little louder this time.

"Sounds wonderful." Liz turned to smile at Alex. "Last week we went to Greece."

"Greece?"

Liz saw his expression and laughed. "Kate didn't tell you that she's taking us on a culinary adventure around the world this summer?"

"No, she didn't."

Alex looked at Kate, who suddenly wouldn't look at *him*.

He moved his bishop before Arthur Lundy put his king in check. For the past five minutes, his opponent had quietly but systematically taken out a knight, three pawns and a rook.

Alex blamed Kate, who was proving to be as distracting as a meteor shower.

"She even plays tour guide and gives us some history of the area." Delia shooed the cat named Lucy off the rocking chair by the window and pulled a skein of bright red yarn out of her bag.

Three teenagers, two girls and a lanky boy Alex remembered seeing at the wedding reception, barged into the apartment. "Did you start yet?"

"Not yet." Kate didn't look at all perturbed by the number of people camped out in her living room.

Come to think of it, the only person she'd looked perturbed to see had been *him*.

She reached for a pitcher on the shelf and the hem of her T-shirt rose a quarter inch, exposing a ribbon of sun-kissed skin.

Alex promptly lost his remaining knight.

"Check." Mr. Lundy grinned.

Alex shook his head in disgust.

"Hi, Mr. Lundy." The girls paused by the coffee table and the one with dark hair stooped down to kiss Arthur's bristly cheek. "Mr. Porter."

Alex was surprised they remembered his name and realized he couldn't return the favor. "Hello..."

"Morgan." The dark-haired girl smiled and pointed to her friend. "This is Haylie."

Instead of politely moving on, they lighted on the arm of the sofa to watch the match, seemingly right at home.

Everyone in Kate's miniscule apartment seemed at home, even though the decibel level and the temperature of the room continued to rise in direct proportion to the number of people streaming in.

Matthew Wilde arrived with two teenage boys in tow, followed by Faye McAllister, who had a purse looped over one arm and a ball of white fluff draped across the other.

The ball of fluff wriggled, jumped down and made a beeline for Ethel and Lucy, who tripled in size as they stared down the intruder. The little dog barked and the cats hissed but Kate didn't appear to be fazed by the commotion. Not only that, the sparkle in her eyes made it look as if she were...enjoying it.

On her way to welcome the newest guests, Kate paused to glance at the chessboard. "You're going to lose your queen," she whispered.

"No, I'm—" Alex stopped.

Yes, he was.

Arthur frowned when Alex blocked his next move. "Would've had you there," he muttered. "But we can finish the game after dinner."

"I can't stay, Mr. Lundy." Alex didn't anticipate his statement would cause such a stir.

Everyone stopped talking and turned to look at him. Even Faye McAllister's yappy little dog quit barking.

"Not staying?" Delia repeated. "You want to go to Italy, don't you?"

"He's probably been there, Delia," Kate murmured.

Twice, but Alex kept that information to himself.

The woman's pink walking cane struck the floor. "Then he can be our tour guide!"

Tour guide?

"I don't think Kate planned on having an extra guest," Alex said carefully.

Emma laughed. "I certainly hope that's not true because we're *all* extra guests."

"And there's lotsa room on the roof," her son, Jeremy, who'd sidled up to watch the match, offered a shy smile.

"The roof?"

"Sure. That's where we eat."

Alex looked at Kate, who met his gaze with a tilt of her chin.

"Kate fixed it up. You'd be surprised at how cozy it is up there." Liz Decker smiled at their hostess.

Surprised by something Kate did? Alex realized that was swiftly becoming a thing of the past.

"And there's plenty of food," Zoey Decker added.

It sounded as if they wanted him to stay. But these were Abby's friends. Kate's friends. He had no connection with the laughing group of people crowded together in the tiny apartment.

You'll find yourself longing for something you never knew you wanted.

"It's your move," Arthur said.

Alex forced a smile and rose to his feet. "I'll take a rain check. I really do have to leave."

While he still remembered why.

Chapter Ten

Kate pedaled up the driveway to the inn, silently reciting the verse she'd chosen to memorize from the book of Proverbs for the coming week.

A word aptly spoken is like apples of gold in settings of silver.

A verse she'd chosen in honor of Alex Porter.

When he'd left so abruptly the day before, she'd actually felt a stab of disappointment. And not only on Arthur's behalf.

A split second before he'd risen to his feet, Kate had seen a flash of indecision in Alex's jade-green eyes. Almost as if a part of him had wanted to stay.

Obviously, a very small part that was easily overridden by his desire not to mingle with the village peasants.

Be nice, Kate.

Funny how often she'd had to repeat those words to herself over the past few days.

Kate hopped off her bicycle and snapped down the kickstand with her heel. Mulligan and Lady ambled up, tails slicing the air, looking way too happy given the fact they were in the care of a man who didn't even pretend to like them.

"Did he make you two sleep outside last night?" She ruffled the cocker spaniel's velvet ears.

Mulligan sat down and barked. Three times.

Be nice, Kate.

"Okay, okay. I will." For Abby's sake, she would pause in the doorway of the office and smile sweetly at Alex on her way to the kitchen…

"There you are."

It would have worked, except that Alex wasn't *in* the office. He stood in the hallway, blocking the way to the kitchen and dressed for battle in lightweight gray slacks, a crisp button-down shirt and a tie.

Kate swallowed a sigh. If she'd known Alex was going to go for the "brooding millionaire executive" look, she would have opted for something a little less casual than a T-shirt, denim capris and tennis shoes.

"Good morning." Like an NFL quarterback, Kate tried to size up the best—and fastest—way around him. She took a step to the side.

So did Alex. "I put a pot of coffee on."

"That was—"

"To save time. Meet me back in the office after you pour yourself a cup."

Now who was finishing the other person's sentences, Kate thought darkly. But she'd promised to be nice, hadn't she? Yes, she had.

"Thank you. I'll be right back."

Her spirits lifted when she walked into the kitchen. Abby had tackled most of the cosmetic changes herself, but she hadn't spared any expense when it came to creating a kitchen that blended down-home charm and cutting-edge technology.

A spacious center island that boasted

double sinks. Natural light from the bank of windows overlooking the garden spilled into the room and winked off the old-fashioned tin ceiling.

The breeze lifted the curtains and stirred the air, carrying the distinct hint of...something burned.

Kate's nose wrinkled. Upon further investigation, she discovered the charred remains of what was once a piece of Abby's homemade oatmeal bread in the wastebasket under the sink.

No wonder Abby and Quinn had questioned Alex's ability to run the *breakfast* part of the bed-and-breakfast.

She hesitated, almost hearing the impatient tap of an Italian leather shoe against the hardwood floor.

But she couldn't let someone go hungry. Not even Alex. Knowing that Abby kept a supply of emergency rations in the freezer, Kate rummaged around until she found something guaranteed to sweeten anyone's mood.

When she paused in the doorway of Abby's

office a few minutes later, Alex stood at the window, staring out at the lake.

Was he wishing he could trade this view for one of the Chicago skyline?

Not Kate. She loved everything about Mirror Lake. She loved the slow pace and familiar faces. She loved that every window acted as a lens for the kaleidoscope of changing seasons, one that transformed the landscape from muted shades of pearl and gray to a shifting palette of greens and blues so clear they almost hurt the eyes before deepening to a fiery display of scarlet, gold and bronze.

Most of all, Kate loved that she had a place here. She *fit*. While the majority of her high school classmates had waited anxiously to kick off the confines of small-town life like a pair of shoes that pinched their feet, Kate had never wanted to leave. When her father had decided to move to Arizona, she jumped at the opportunity to take over the café.

Only once had Kate regretted her decision. One brief moment in time that she'd wished she were someone else. Some*thing* else.

Kate took a deep breath and carefully tucked away the memory with the same resolve she had the first time it had sneaked through her defenses.

The day she'd met Alex Porter.

Kate cleared her throat to get Alex's attention before stepping into the office.

"I warmed up a few of Abby's blueberry scones."

Alex rotated to face her, his gaze dropping to the china plate Kate set down on the desk. "You didn't have breakfast?"

"Of course I did. It's the most important meal of the day."

Alex's eyebrows met over the bridge of his nose. "You don't have to feed me."

"I found evidence to the contrary."

A wry smile hooked the corner of his lips. "That was collateral damage. I was trying to find the coffee."

Kate refused to be charmed by Alex Porter's...charm. This, she sternly reminded herself, was the man who'd rebuffed her friends' invitation to stay for dinner and walked out of her apartment without a backward glance.

Alex wasn't always like this. He had a lot of friends before our parents put us in private school. He loved to play practical jokes when we were kids.

Kate couldn't remember where she put her car keys half the time, so why did she remember everything Abby had said about her older brother?

Alex claimed the chair behind the desk, snagged a scone and got straight down to business.

"I went over the list of reservations. Charles and Irene Gibson will be checking into one of the cabins this afternoon. They'll be staying through the weekend.

"Thursday there will be a couple on their honeymoon, two cabins booked with kayak enthusiasts, one who is lactose-intolerant, and a single guest who requested a vegetarian option…are you listening, Kate? Don't you think you should be writing this down?"

"Yes." Alex didn't have to know Kate's response had been directed to the second question. Because, if she were truly honest, the answer to the first would have been, *"No, I got distracted by your eyelashes again…"*

Swallowing hard, she fished a pen and notebook out of her backpack.

"Lactose. Vegetarian. Kayaks." As Kate jotted down the information, she became aware that Alex had gone completely still. She looked up. "What is it?"

"It's...pink." It was the first thing that popped into Alex's head. Except that he didn't usually *say* the first thing that popped into his head.

But...he'd expected Kate to tug a laptop out of her backpack. Or a neat, professional-looking leather binder. Not a hot pink, spiral-bound notebook and a pen encrusted with so much bling that it resembled a Fourth of July float.

"I know. The girls in my book club like to give me sparkly things on my birthday." Kate swiped at the pom-pom dancing on the end of the cap. "I think it's sweet. Is there anything else?"

Alex managed to yank his gaze free from the slow, hypnotic movement of the glitter floating inside of the pen's cartridge.

"When the guests check in, Abby gives them a choice as to whether they want a continental breakfast delivered right to their cabin or if they prefer to join the other guests in the dining room."

He handed her a sheet of paper lined with organized, typewritten notes. "Abby acts as the dining room hostess but I can hire someone if you prefer."

"I'm already here," she pointed out. "It won't be any trouble to serve breakfast and keep the coffee going."

"I ordered a new oven. It will be here by tomorrow afternoon." Alex leaned back in the chair, expecting to see profound relief on Kate's face. What he saw looked a lot like… horror?

"You can't get rid of Mrs. Avocado!"

"Who is Mrs. Avocado?"

"Abby's oven."

"My sister *named* the oven?"

"Mrs. Avocado is not just an oven." Kate leaped to her feet. "She's an…an icon."

"No, she's—" Alex stopped and shook his head. "I mean *it's,* a temperamental green dinosaur that isn't worth the price I'm paying to have it shipped to the junkyard."

Kate slapped both hands on the desk and leaned forward until Alex got a close-up of a tiny, star-shaped freckle just below the corner of her left eye.

"It works if a person knows what they're doing!"

He leaned forward, too. "I know exactly what I'm doing. I'm running the inn."

"And I'm running the *kitchen*. I say we don't need a new oven." A spiral of copper hair flopped down over Kate's eye, blocking the star-shaped freckle from Alex's view.

Their fingers tangled as they attempted to brush it away. At the same time.

Alex's lungs stopped working as he stared down at Kate. He'd always been good at reading people...but he was suddenly afraid of what he might see in her eyes. And what she might see in his.

A low laugh shocked them apart—yanking their attention to the doorway, where an elderly couple stood grinning. Two short, round bookends in matching white polo shirts, Bermuda shorts and straw hats.

"Mr. and Mrs. Gibson?" Alex managed to find his voice.

"That's us!" the woman sang out.

Her husband's face split into a sly grin.

"And I can tell from the way you two are looking at each other that you must be the newlyweds!"

"You and Charlie *have* to spend a few days there when you get a chance, my friend, Lydia, said." Irene Gibson kicked a pinecone and sent it spinning off the path as she and Kate trudged toward the cabins. "'Mirror Lake is one of the most peaceful places on earth.'"

"Uh-huh." That didn't sound too convincing, so Kate tried again. "It is peaceful."

At least it had been. Up until Alex Porter descended on the place like the plagues of Egypt all rolled into one inflexible, infuriating man. A man who happened to have a smile that melted her defenses.

"I would have liked to meet Abby," Irene prattled on. "She made Lydia and Simon's fiftieth wedding anniversary so special by letting them renew their vows here last summer."

Kate winced as the woman's suitcase— shaped like a ladybug but certainly heavier than one—bumped against her bare ankle.

"Abby is one of my closest friends. I can vouch for the fact that she is a real sweetheart."

Irene's head bobbed up and down, rattling the cluster of fake cherries pinned to the crown of her hat. "Her brother seems to be, too."

Kate stumbled. "Alex?"

"Oh." Two penciled eyebrows dipped together to form a crooked line above the bridge of her nose. "Does she have more than one?"

"No…" But still.

"He's quite easy on the eyes, I must say." Irene's voice dropped to a whisper. "Charlie was quite the looker when he was that age. One smile and I was a goner."

"That's very…romantic." And hopefully, Kate thought a little desperately, impossible.

"How long have you two been dating?"

"Dating? No. Alex and I…we aren't…" *Come on. Spit it out, Kate!* "We work together. Temporarily. We barely know each other."

Irene didn't seem to hear her. "The moment I met Charlie, I knew he was the one. He proposed two weeks later and I never looked back."

Looking back wasn't the issue. It was looking ahead. A relationship with Alex would be impossible. He lived and worked in Chicago. He wasn't simply *on* the A-list, he made up the list. And he avoided relationships the way a person would avoid a communicable disease.

Because of his past.

"Don't," Kate muttered.

It wasn't an excuse. Alex and Abby had both experienced the pain of losing someone they loved, but Abby had turned to God for healing. Alex had defaulted to his Grand Plan.

Irene clucked her tongue and the cherries on her hat wagged back and forth sympathetically. "I tried to talk myself out of it, too. It didn't work."

Kate had to try one more time. "Believe me, Mrs. Gibson, Alex and I have *nothing* in common. When you and your husband saw us—" she hesitated, then decided that the only way to nip this crazy idea in the bud was to be honest. Totally, brutally honest. "Well, we were right in the middle of a disagreement. Something that happens a lot, I might add."

To Kate's chagrin, the woman let out a merry laugh.

"You might have been in the middle of something, Miss Nichols, but trust me, from where I stood it *wasn't* a disagreement."

Chapter Eleven

Alex opened a cabinet door and came face to face with another heart-shaped sticky note, waiting for him like a fluorescent pink booby trap.

"Abby," he growled his sister's name, although she was thousands of miles away.

Alex wasn't sure if the Bible verses he'd been finding tucked in odd places around the inn were meant for him or if they had something to do with Abby's newfound faith. Knowing her, it was probably both.

He skimmed the words and frowned.

"What good is it for a man to gain the whole world, yet lose or forfeit his very self?"

Alex shut the door but the question clung

to his thoughts like the adhesive on the back of the paper.

Was it wrong to work hard? To finish what his parents had started?

In a way, Alex had gained the "whole world." But it had never been about money. Or possessions. Those were a by-product of a promise he had made to himself after their parents died. Neither one of those things stemmed from a desire to build a reputation for himself, but to continue to live up to the one he had been entrusted with.

How could that be a bad thing?

"Our parents built walls to protect us, Alex, but they're not as thick as the one you've built around your heart to protect yourself."

He could still see the look in Abby's eyes the day she turned in her resignation. Not anger, not bitterness, but pity.

"I'm tired of living like this." Abby had reached for his hand. *"I want to be free."*

Free from what? Alex had wanted to ask.

Abby was walking away from a lifestyle the majority of people could only dream about; and yet, she felt sorry for him.

It hadn't made sense at the time.

"It still doesn't make sense," Alex muttered. "She gave up everything."

And she seemed at peace.

That didn't make sense, either.

When Alex's cell phone rang, he snatched it up as if it were a lifeline.

"Porter—"

"Is Kate there?" a lilting, feminine voice wanted to know.

"What?"

"I'd like to talk to Kate," the voice repeated, enunciating each word this time.

"Who is this?"

"Missy Martin. I'm a waitress at the café."

Right. The blond, perky teenager who'd wanted more hours. "This is my private number, Missy."

"I know," the girl said cheerfully. "I tried to call the inn but no one answered. And Kate forgets her cell phone *everywhere*. I called Abby and she gave me your number."

She called— "Abby is in Paris."

"Uh-huh." Missy giggled. "She and Quinn are having a great time and she said to tell you hi. So, *hi*."

An expectant pause followed.

"Oh." Alex closed his eyes, feeling a little ridiculous but knowing there was only one thing that would move the conversation toward a swift and satisfying conclusion. "Hi."

Half-hearted, Alex knew, but it seemed to satisfy her. "I'm not sure where Kate is at the—"

"That's okay. I can't talk long anyway, Zach and I are going canoeing this afternoon. Will you give Kate a message for me?"

"A message?"

"Yes. A message." Missy raised her voice until she was practically shouting into the phone, making Alex feel as if he were as old as Rip Van Winkle. He had no one to blame but himself, asking her to repeat half the things she'd said.

"You could always leave a voicemail," Alex suggested. "On *her* phone."

"Kate doesn't check her voicemail, either."

And apparently sarcasm did not stick to the Teflon coating of Missy Martin's sunny personality.

He gave in. "What's the message?"

"Do you have a pen?"

"Yes." Alex was tempted to add that he also had four hotels and a master's degree in business. That, when added together, gave him the ability to remember a simple phone message.

"The youth group girls are having a make-over party tomorrow night and Kate's invited."

"Makeover?"

"Right. *Makeover.* That's when a bunch of girls get together and play with cool makeup and do their hair and—"

"I know what a makeover is, Missy."

"Awesome." Missy sounded impressed. "And tell Kate to bring her killer cappuccino brownies."

"Okay—"

"And a movie. Maybe *Ever After.* Or *The Princess Bride.*"

"Killer brownies. Movies. I'll pass that on." Along with a few suggestions about cell phone responsibility.

"Thanks a lot, Mr. Porter. 'Bye!"

Alex slid the phone into his back pocket and headed down to the lake, where Charlie and Irene Gibson were dangling their feet over the side of the dock.

The couple turned to him with matching smiles.

"Mr. Porter! Kick off your shoes and join us!" Charlie said. "The water is beautiful."

"And you're way too buttoned up for a day like this," his wife chimed in.

Alex resisted the urge to pluck at the silk tie around his neck. "I appreciate the invitation, but I can't right now. I'm looking for Kate."

"Two boys showed up a little while ago and they disappeared into the woods." Irene pointed beyond the cabins, where a thick stand of mature white pine hemmed the shoreline.

"Kate went with them?

"She was carrying something. I assumed the boys needed help."

Then they should have taken a number. Missy wanted cappuccino brownies and two movies that Alex could no longer remember the names of. And *he* needed to post the breakfast menu for the guests that would be arriving tomorrow.

"That young woman is a gem. I know one

when I see one." Charlie cast an adoring look at the woman sitting beside him. "Proverbs thirty-one says, 'A wife of noble character, who can find? She is worth far more than rubies.'"

It was a conspiracy. Alex cast a wary glance up at the sky, wondering if the next thing he would see was a skywriter weaving a Bible verse between the clouds.

Irene noticed Alex's expression and smiled. "A mother is giving her son, the king, advice on what qualities to look for in a wife."

Advice that might be helpful if he was looking for a wife. But, right now, Alex happened to be looking for a stubborn, outspoken redhead…who had the most intriguing freckle under her left eye.

His heart cinched at the memory of their recent argument. Alex wasn't *used* to having people argue with him. Having a conversation with Kate was like trying to navigate a raft down a river. A river filled with unexpected twists and turns. Hidden obstacles.

It was frustrating.

Exhilarating…

Alex sucked in a breath.

Impossible.

"Mr. Porter?" The voice seemed to come from far away, echoing through a long corridor and eventually finding Alex frozen in the midst of his panic.

He stared at Charlie Gibson. "I'm sorry. Did you say something?"

Charlie nudged his wife.

"What did I tell you?" he whispered.

Irene nodded sagely. "You're right every time."

There was no way Alex was going to ask what the man was right about every time. No way at all.

"I don't think this one is going to work." Kate wedged her foot more firmly into a notch in the tree trunk and peered up at the grid of branches above her head.

"Are you sure?" Jeremy Sutton squinted up at her, his face solemn. "My calculations were based on the circumference of the trees and the distribution of the weight of the platform on the lower branches."

Kate ducked her head to hide a smile. "And I'm sure those calculations would have been fine—if a Pileated woodpecker hadn't weakened the entire structure of this particular tree."

The boys exhaled in mutual adolescent frustration.

"Now what do we do?" Cody wanted to know.

Jeremy sighed. "Revise the plans. Again."

"Thomas Edison made nine hundred and ninety-nine attempts before he invented the light bulb." Kate liked to put a positive spin on things.

"Thomas Edison didn't have school," Jeremy pointed out.

"Or woodpeckers," Cody added glumly.

"I have confidence in you boys. You'll figure something out." Kate inched her way down to the next branch, heard another snap and dropped to the ground, glad she'd intercepted the boys when she saw them heading the woods with a load of lumber.

At her apartment the day before, Jeremy had mentioned that he and Cody were planning to build a tree fort but Kate didn't realize that Abby had offered the use of her property.

And even though Alex had been sitting two feet away at the time, she had her doubts that he did, either. She'd have to wait for the right time to let him know what the boys were up to.

Maybe when Alex was safely back in Chicago.

A squirrel scampered up the tree beside her and crouched on a nearby limb, chattering a warning.

Mulligan lifted his nose and let out a warning bark.

"What do you hear, buddy?" From her vantage point above the ground, Kate caught a glimpse of something moving through the brush.

"Oh, no." She closed her eyes, hoping it was a figment of her imagination.

"What is it?" Jeremy sounded a little worried. "A bear?"

"Worse," Kate muttered.

"A wolf?"

If only. "It's—"

"Mr. Porter!" Jeremy grinned as the intruder stepped into the clearing.

Oh, the innocence of children, Kate

thought. She would have preferred the bear. Or even the wolf. But it was Alex, a man who understood hotels, not tree forts.

Alex's gaze swept over the boys, the mismatched pile of lumber, and Kate, who pressed her back against the trunk of the tree and wished she had the ability to blend into her surroundings like a tree frog.

"Kate?"

She tipped her head, completely fascinated by the number of questions Alex could contain in a single word. She decided to answer the easiest one.

"I was helping the boys pick out a spot for their tree fort."

"Doesn't Abby own this land?"

"You did it again," Kate breathed, impressed in spite of the fact they were probably in big trouble.

"Quinn said we could build it here." Jeremy spoke up. "Me and Cody live in town and Mayor Dodd says the trees in the park belong to everyone—"

"And have to remain in their natural state," Cody finished.

Kate couldn't help but smile at the boy's

spot-on imitation of the mayor's booming voice.

"Don't you think this is a cool place for a fort, Mr. Porter?" Jeremy searched Alex's face, his expression earnest.

"We even drew up the plans." Mustering his courage, Cody handed Alex a black notebook.

Kate sidled closer and couldn't prevent a tiny gasp from escaping.

When she and her friends had built a tree fort back in elementary school, they'd hammered a few boards in place to create a platform. Attached the extra pieces to the trunk of the tree to make a ladder.

Jeremy and Cody's version was a bit more…elaborate. A *Swiss Family Robinson* getaway, complete with a pulley system, multiple platforms and something that looked suspiciously like—

"A suspension bridge." Jeremy grinned. "That was my idea."

Kate slid a glance at Alex. She could almost see visions of injuries and lawsuits dancing in his head.

"But Kate climbed up first and said we

shouldn't use these trees." The toe of Jeremy's tennis shoe ground a circle in the moss. "Because the structure of the center one has been compromised."

Cody heaved a sigh. "Woodpeckers."

Alex slowly pivoted to face her. "You climbed the tree?"

Kate reminded herself that she had to act as a positive role model for the boys and tell the truth. No matter what the consequences.

"I wanted to make sure it was safe."

"And it wasn't."

"Well…" Kate sensed she was treading on dangerous ground. If she didn't know better, she would have thought Alex was concerned about her. "Someone had to test it out."

"You don't like heights."

She opened her mouth to disagree but Alex gave her a look. A look telling her that he remembered the night she'd been stranded on the roof of the gazebo.

Kate lifted her chin. "I don't like boys climbing potentially dangerous trees even more."

Alex stalked over to the largest oak for a better look. To her surprise, the boys trailed behind him, not at all put off by the grim expression on his face.

"Abby said we could sleep out here and everything," Cody said, unable to hide his excitement.

"We're going to have a skylight for my tele-scope—"

"And bunk beds."

"No," Alex said flatly. "This isn't going to work."

The boys' faces fell, leaving Kate in charge of damage control. Frustration surged through her. Did Alex have to be so cold and matter-of-fact about everything? Didn't he know that the rest of the human race—in-cluding adolescent boys—had feelings?

"Wait until Abby and Quinn get back. Or better yet, Alex can call them to verify that you have permission." Kate wrapped a com-forting arm around Jeremy's thin shoulders and glared at Alex for good measure.

He didn't notice because he was looking at Jeremy's blueprint again.

"I mean the *plan* won't work," he mur-mured. "In this type of design, you're going to want to use the two trees on this side, not the center one, as weight-bearing walls. Then it doesn't matter if the woodpeckers turned this tree into an all-you-can-eat buffet."

Jeremy and Cody crowded closer and the younger boy's face lit up. "He's right."

"And if you put the suspension bridge here…" Alex traced the tip of his index finger along the drawing. "You can have a balcony on this side. That should give you a pretty good view of the lake."

Kate blinked. She'd thought the suspension bridge sounded questionable and Alex was actually suggesting they add a balcony?

"Sweet!" the boys grinned at each other.

"You'll have to put rails around it, though."

Two blond heads nodded vigorously. "We will."

"So, you're saying it's all right with you if they build the fort?" Kate had to be missing something here.

"Yes—" Alex waited until the whoops died down. "But there are going to be rules."

Of course. Kate almost breathed a sigh of relief. This was the Alex Porter she knew and loved.

Whoa. Not loved. The Alex Porter she knew and…*knew.*

"First, you have to check in with me whenever you're going to work out here. And it has to be during the day." Alex ignored the disappointed look that passed between the two boys. "I want a daily progress report and if you have any more design problems, you'll come and talk to me before you keep going. Agreed?"

"Agreed."

"And if you get hungry or thirsty, come to the kitchen for a glass of lemonade and cookies." Kate had her own set of rules.

"Mom packed us lunches today, but she said you'd probably have dessert." Jeremy grinned.

Emma knew her too well…

"Lunch!" Kate choked out. "What time is it?"

Jeremy consulted his cell phone. "Eleven thirty."

"I have to get back to the café." Grady was going to wonder what on earth happened had happened to her.

Kate had promised to be back in time to

serve the lunch crowd, but between the Gibsons' early arrival and helping the boys tote lumber to the site of their fort, she had totally lost track of the time. "I'll stop back later and see how you're coming along."

"Thanks, Kate." The boys waved but she could see their attention was focused once again on the notebook.

To her surprise, Alex fell into step beside her, his stride comfortable and fluid, as if he were navigating a city sidewalk instead of trekking through the forest.

"Thanks for letting them build the fort," Kate finally ventured. "It means a lot to the boys, especially Cody. He doesn't have much of a home life, so this will be good for him."

"Abby and Quinn were the ones who gave them permission," Alex said curtly. "I'm still not convinced it's a good idea."

"They're very responsible, and I'm sure Jake will be here to help when he's not on duty."

"I'll talk to him. They're going to need help when it's time to make that bridge." The sudden glint of humor in Alex's eyes gave

Kate the courage to ask the question that had been nagging her for the past ten minutes.

"How do you know so much about tree forts?"

He pulled ahead of her, forcing Kate to vault over a fallen log to keep up.

"Oh, I'm sorry," she gasped. "Is that classified information?"

Alex gave in and smiled.

"I got my undergrad in architecture."

Chapter Twelve

"Architecture?"

Alex ducked his head to avoid being strangled by a skein of wild grapevine that Kate skipped right under. "You sound surprised."

"I assumed your degree would be in business. Or hotel management."

It might have been. If Alex's original plan had been to follow in his father's footsteps.

He shrugged. "Building is building, whether it's a high-rise apartment complex or a reputation for being the best."

At least that's what he'd told himself when he took control of his parents' hotels after their death.

Kate was silent for a moment, and then, "But being an architect was your dream."

The quiet statement felt like the thrust of a knife between his ribs. Alex didn't want to talk about his dreams. Or the past.

"What about you?" In the interest of self-preservation, he turned the tables on her. "Was it your *dream* to own a café in Mirror Lake?"

"From the time I was six years old and made my first piecrust from scratch." Kate's lips curved in a smile. "My parents would take me to work with them and let me mess around in the kitchen. In high school, I went in early to help with the breakfast shift and worked weekends, doing everything from waiting tables to bookkeeping."

Kate had learned the family business from the ground up while Alex had had it dropped into his lap. He didn't resent having to change direction after his parents died, but he'd been determined to chart his own course from that moment on. Maintaining tight boundaries, personally and professionally, he had reduced the number of outside variables.

And pain.

Alex shifted the conversation to safer ground. "Where is your dad now?"

"He lives in Arizona. After I graduated, Dad started talking about moving to a warmer climate. He has asthma and the winters were getting harder on him. He tried to get me to apply to colleges out there, but I realized that I wanted to be *here*.

"He finally agreed to let me take over the café on a one-year trial basis so I would know for sure if it was what I wanted."

Alex didn't have to ask what Kate's decision had been. But he couldn't believe she was still content with it.

"Grady helped and I use a lot of the recipes Mom handed down."

"You've never taken cooking classes?"

"No." Kate slanted a look at him, a mischievous sparkle in her eyes. "But I teach them during the winter. The Art of Making a Piecrust from Scratch and Meat loaf 101."

"You could be doing more," Alex said bluntly.

"More?" From the puzzled expression on Kate's face, she had no idea what he meant. Alex felt obligated to clarify.

"You could be doing more than serving people blueberry pie and coffee."

For a moment, the only sound was the muffled tread of their footsteps on the forest floor.

"It sounds like you think I'm settling."

"Aren't you?"

Kate stopped walking and whirled around to face him, hands parked on her slender hips. "I settled *down*. In a place that I love. And I'm doing what I love. Can you say the same thing?"

Held captive by her gaze, Alex felt something shift inside him.

Could he?

Over the past few months he'd been feeling...restless. Not the kind of restlessness that in the past had prompted Alex to research places to build a new hotel or invest in stock guaranteed to turn a healthy profit.

This, Alex sensed, went deeper. To places he was reluctant to explore.

Maybe he should blame his sister. He'd been so sure he could convince Abby to return to Chicago. Sure that he knew what was best for her. But the summer before when he'd visited Mirror Lake, determined to make Abby see that being an innkeeper wasn't a good fit for her, Alex had been surprised to find she had changed.

The sister he'd tried so hard to shelter had claimed she was living in the shelter of God's wings, and Mirror Lake was where she was supposed to be.

Alex hadn't been able to dismiss the peace in Abby's eyes as easily as he had dismissed the words. He'd returned to Chicago alone. Nothing had changed, but something felt... different.

Empty.

At first he thought he was adjusting to Abby's absence, but they talked more often now than they ever did. Not only were the hotels doing well, but a few weeks ago, a real estate agent had hinted that Alex might be interested in a prime piece of property going up for sale on a lake just minutes from the city.

Ordinarily, Alex, who thrived on a challenge, would have looked into purchasing the land immediately. Instead, he'd offered to stay in Mirror Lake for two weeks.

What good is it for a man to gain the whole world and lose himself or his very soul?

And the challenge had taken the form of a question Alex was no longer sure he knew the answer to.

"Never mind." Kate started walking again.

Why had she expected him to understand?

Alex Porter had everything on the world's checklist for success. Money. Looks. Influence. Reputation.

Cars with engines that worked.

But he doesn't have peace.

Ohh. Kate didn't want to hear that still, small voice again. The one that reminded her Alex was a human being. A human being that God loved and was reaching out to—the way He loved her and had drawn her to Himself when she was a child.

Kate's hands curled at her sides.

Sometimes she had the strangest feeling that holding on to her anger was the only thing that prevented her from reaching out to Alex.

But that would be a mistake on so

many levels, Kate couldn't even begin to count them.

The silence between them was shattered by the sound of Alex's cell phone.

"Porter."

Kate increased her pace. This was good timing. While Alex took the call, she could sprint to her bicycle...

"It's for you."

"Me?" Kate squeaked.

"At least I don't have to take a message this time." Alex handed her his cell.

This time?

"Hello?" Kate stammered, aware that Alex was tuned into every word.

"Thank goodness, Kate!" Mrs. Kadinsky's voice crackled in her ear. "My grandchildren are driving up for the day and the café is completely out of your caramel apple pie. You know it's the twins' favorite."

"I'm sorry." Kate understood the seriousness of the woman's predicament. Mrs. Kadinsky doted on her grandchildren. "Why don't you call Grady at the café and ask if we have one or two in the freezer?"

"I already did and the only thing he could

find was blueberry." A sigh rolled out. "They'll be sooo disappointed."

Kate silently scrolled through the rest of her day. She had a few hours between the lunch shift and the time she had to report back to the inn.

"I can whip up a few."

"Really, Kate? You are a lifesaver. That would be wonderful!"

"No problem, Mrs. K. I'll drop them off at your house later this afternoon." Kate handed the phone back to Alex, saw his scowl—which did nothing to detract from his looks—and started the countdown.

Three. Two. One…

"Unbelievable." Alex practically growled the word. "You have to work at the café this afternoon and then come back here to make breakfast for the Gibsons tomorrow. Tomorrow night there's a makeover party tomorrow at nine—bring your killer brownies, by the way—and now you're offering to bake pies for sweet little old ladies."

Obviously, Alex had never met Mrs. Kadinsky, a retired parole officer from Milwaukee. The woman was six feet tall and had won the log-throwing contest during the Reflection Day celebration four years in a row…

Wait a second. The rest of what Alex had said suddenly sank in.

Makeover party? Kate had almost forgotten about that.

A thought suddenly occurred to her. "You looked in my planner!"

"No, I've been taking your phone messages," Alex retorted.

"You don't carry your cell, so Missy called me instead—"

The smile that worked its way to the surface died a quick death as Alex continued.

"—You do too much."

Kate stumbled to a halt again and stared at Alex in disbelief. "Two minutes ago, you said that I should be doing more!"

"I meant more for *yourself,* not for the town."

Kate thought of all the people who had invested so much in her life after she'd lost her mother. Women like Esther Redstone and Liz Decker, who had prayed, not just with her but *for* her. Two of the many women whose advice Kate treasured. Women who had talked her out of dyeing her hair black and helped her choose a dress for the senior prom.

Not to mention the faithful customers who had cheered for her when she'd taken over the café at the tender age of twenty.

"It's the same thing."

"I have no idea what you're talking about."

That's because they weren't speaking the same language, Kate thought—once again acutely aware of the differences between them.

"The people who live in Mirror Lake are like an extended family to me," she explained, asking God for an extra measure of patience. "They aren't *taking* anything."

Not anything that she didn't freely give, anyway. Yes, she was busy. God had blessed her with energy and creativity to do His work. When Kate felt depleted, she rested in His presence and drew from His strength.

"Really? Because from where I stand, it looks like they're taking advantage of you."

"Then maybe you need to get closer."

"That's where you're wrong. The trouble is, you get *too* close. If you were one of my managers, the first thing you'd learn is how to keep a professional distance from the people you come into contact with."

"You're offering me a job?" Kate asked tartly.

"What if I am?"

"I'd say no!"

Wouldn't she?

For a split second, Kate's traitorous imagination conjured up an image of seeing Alex every day. And instead of picturing herself running for cover, something warm lit within her.

Something that had the potential to burn out of control, leaving behind wounds that could take years to heal.

If they healed at all.

She mentally shook herself, knowing Alex hadn't been serious.

"Look at me." Kate laughed. "I wouldn't fit in."

She hadn't meant for him to take the words literally. But his gaze swept over her, from the Little Orphan Annie curls to the scuffed canvas tennis shoes on her feet.

"No," he said softly. "You wouldn't."

Of course, *now* he agreed with her.

Kate opened her mouth to make a snappy comeback, but something in his expression stopped her.

Because she had the strangest feeling that Alex had just paid her a compliment.

"I'm looking out my window at the Eiffel Tower. What are you looking at?"

Alex yanked his gaze away from the petite figure gamboling down the shoreline, backlit by the moon.

"Trees," he said truthfully.

"I miss trees." Abby sighed.

"They'll be here when you get back." Alex stepped back and let the curtain fall into place, blocking Kate from view.

"How are you and Kate getting along?" Abby's innocent question brought out a rueful smile. It seemed there was no escaping Kate, after all.

"It's only been twenty-four hours."

"I repeat—" Laughter rippled below the surface of the words.

"She helped the Gibsons make a campfire tonight." Even though it wasn't part of her job description. "Tomorrow evening she plans to teach them how to paddle a canoe."

Again, not in her job description.

"Sometimes I wish I could bottle Kate's energy. She practically runs the entire town."

Alex didn't want to talk about Kate. Because it only made him *think* about Kate.

He leaned a hip into the side of the desk and studied an amateur watercolor centered on the wall. "So how is Paris?"

"It's better when you're with someone you love," Abby said in a dreamy voice.

"You could look up Millicent Carstairs while you're there. She's the designer I hired last month and she has a portfolio of her work for the ballroom renovations—"

"I'm on my honeymoon, Alex."

"So take Quinn with you. I'm sure Ms. Carstairs wouldn't mind another opinion."

"Goodbye, Alex!"

"Let me know if you change your—" He was talking to dead air. His baby sister had hung up on him.

Laughing, Alex heard the door close as Kate left.

He tried not to let it bother him that she

hadn't come in to tell him that she was leaving. After all, he'd avoided her all evening, closing himself in the office to do paperwork while she worked in the kitchen.

Making sure the lines of division remained firmly in place.

Mulligan and Lady trotted past the doorway and Alex remembered another promise he'd made to his sister.

"Come on, you two. Time for the last walk of the day."

The dogs ignored him and continued on, as if someone had set them on a mission.

Reminded once again why he preferred fake houseplants to living creatures, Alex followed.

By the time he reached the kitchen, Mulligan and Lady lay stretched out on the rug in front of the sink, gnawing on biscuits roughly the size of a shoebox.

They actually smelled good, too. Reminding him that he'd worked through supper.

Alex opened the refrigerator, hoping to find some chicken leftover from the reception. What he saw was a plate piled high with food. Meat loaf, mashed potatoes and gravy, and green beans. A slice of blueberry pie, so large it drooped over the sides of the plate, sat on the rack above it.

Before he could change his mind, Alex punched in a number on his cell.

"Thank you."

For a moment, the absolute silence made him wonder if he'd called the wrong person. But there was no mistaking the laugh, husky with surprise, that followed.

"Not too plebeian for your tastes?"

"I'm starving." Alex removed the plate from the fridge and slid it into the microwave.

"That doesn't answer my question, but I figured you might be," Kate said drily. "You didn't come out of the office all evening."

Alex didn't point out that she hadn't left the kitchen, either. Not until she'd slipped out of the main lodge to deliver a bowl of popcorn and a pitcher of lemonade to the Gibsons' cabin.

Alex sent his staff to expensive corporate training events to cultivate that kind of attention to detail, a quality that seemed to come as naturally to Kate as breathing. He was amazed at the way she took care of people.

The way she was taking care of him right now.

"The Gibsons want breakfast delivered to their cabin in the morning, so I'll be back at five," Kate told him.

"You must be looking forward to putting your feet up."

"I have a city council meeting at eight but they only last a few hours."

"I can't believe that in a town the size of Mirror Lake that it would last more than five minutes."

Instead of taking offense, Kate chuckled. "You'd be surprised."

The sound went straight through Alex, cutting a path through his defenses and making him forget why he'd decided it was best to keep his distance from a certain sassy, red-headed café owner.

"What's on the agenda for tonight?" The timer went off and Alex plucked Kate's apron from the hook on the wall, wrapped it around his hand and used it to remove the steaming plate from the microwave.

"Our annual Reflection Day celebration is coming up in September. There's a parade on the lake. Craft and food booths in the park. A lot of planning goes into it."

"And a lot of work." Alex propped open the door of the fridge with one shoulder and reached for the pitcher of lemonade.

"That, too. But it's fun."

Fun? Alex didn't think he'd ever used the words "fun" and "meeting" in the same sentence before.

A moment of silence stretched between them, but it was the comfortable kind. The same thought must have occurred to Kate.

"Wow." She sounded bemused. "I think we're actually having a conversation instead of an argument."

"That isn't possible," Alex said firmly.

"Of course it is."

Silence. And then Kate's laughter started where his ended, linking them together.

"Maybe you're right. We're arguing about the fact that we aren't arguing."

Alex realized he was still smiling as he sat down at the table.

He heard a car door slam in the background

and then a chorus of voices, telling him that Kate had reached her destination.

"I'll see you tomorrow. Have a nice dinner," she murmured.

Alex was used to eating alone. Preferred it most of the time. But as he hung up the phone, he realized that something was missing—something that would have made the evening a lot more enjoyable.

Kate's company.

That scared him more than the green beans.

Chapter Thirteen

❧

"Hey, Kate! You forgot something!"

At the sound of Haylie Owens's voice, Kate glanced over her shoulder and saw the teenager dashing across the church parking lot to catch up to her, waving her cell phone.

She braked and turned Penelope around. "Thanks. I wouldn't have noticed it was gone until tomorrow morning."

Haylie grinned. "I would miss mine if I set it down for five minutes. Mom says it's superglued to my hand."

"I'll see you on Sunday." Kate reached for the purse looped over her shoulder but Haylie leaped forward, a horrified look on her face.

"Careful! You don't want to wreck your manicure."

No, Kate planned to assign that task to the bottle of nail polish remover stashed in her linen cabinet. One of the girls at the makeover party had painted Kate's nails with a color called Ocean Waves, a sickly shade of bluish-green that she had secretly dubbed Sea Sick.

It matched her eye shadow perfectly.

"I had a lot of fun tonight. And the brownies were awesome!" Haylie jogged backward a few steps and the light from the streetlamp glinted off the rhinestone barrettes in her hair. "Rob's picking me up in a few minutes. I wonder if he'll recognize me."

"He might not." Kate wouldn't have that problem. Even with false eyelashes, a thick veneer of foundation covering her freckles and her curls held captive by a large, tortoiseshell clip, Kate knew she would still resemble one of Santa's elves.

A pickup truck swung into the parking lot and stopped long enough for Haylie to climb into it. Kate unzipped her purse and was about to drop her phone inside when the tiny screen lit up.

Three missed calls.

Kate scrolled through them.

Alex Porter. Alex Porter and...Alex Porter.

Three in a row. Each one approximately, oh, let's see, thirty-two seconds apart.

That could only mean one thing.

He'd seen the flyers.

Should she call him back?

Kate glanced at her watch and decided against it. It was almost eleven o'clock, so Alex would just have to wait until morning for a full explanation, that was all there was to it.

Kate felt a pang of regret that the brief—very brief—cease fire they'd enjoyed on the phone the previous night was about to come to a screeching halt.

Because Alex had released his inner despot and made an executive decision to cancel the afternoon tea on Thursday and Kate had... well, she'd *vetoed* it, that's what she had done.

No matter what Alex thought, it was too late to cancel. Kate had already planned the menu and Zoey had offered to play the piano while Emma helped her serve. Her friends were almost as excited about the event as the guests who'd reserved a table.

Before Kate had left the inn for the day, she'd tacked up one or two—*possibly ten*— flyers to remind the guests of the upcoming event.

Now she battled a niggling sense of guilt. Maybe if Alex had given her a good reason *why* he'd made the decision, she wouldn't have taken matters into her own hands.

I'm canceling it.

That's all he'd said. If Kate had chosen a more subtle way to say "No, you're not," it was only because she was shorter than him by a foot and didn't have the innate ability to raise one eyebrow.

A girl had to work with the gifts she'd been given.

Kate pedaled down Main Street and coasted through the alley behind the café, hoping she could make it up to her apartment without being seen. Not only were her curls now waging war against the hairclip, one of the false eyelashes had come unglued and was flapping against her cheek like a loose shutter.

Her cell phone began to vibrate inside her bag and Kate blew out a sigh.

Was the man nocturnal?

She ignored it, letting it jump around inside her purse as she unlocked the door and let herself into the apartment. Catching a glimpse of herself in the antique mirror hanging above the coat rack, Kate winced.

Just as she'd suspected. She looked as if she'd wrestled with a rainbow. And lost.

Ethel and Lucy wandered up to greet her, not at all put off by the new disguise.

The cell gave one final, indignant chirp and was silent. Finally. She changed into her favorite pair of sweats and was attempting to peel off the remaining eyelash without removing the real one underneath when the phone rang again.

"Fine," she muttered, tracking the sound back to her purse and flipped it open without looking at the number. If he really wanted a showdown at midnight rather than high noon...

"Thank goodness," a voice said.

A voice that didn't belong to Alex.

* * *

The smell of bacon frying lured Alex to the kitchen.

"Good morning, Mr. Porter!"

Alex stopped short at the sight of Irene Gibson sashaying around the kitchen, a colorful apron knotted around the waist of her denim jumper.

"Mrs. Gibson." His gaze bounced from the bowls lined up on the counter to the bacon sizzling in the cast-iron skillet on the stove.

"How are you doing this morning?"

He'd been doing fine. Until now. "Where is Kate?"

Humming under her breath, Mrs. Gibson opened the oven door and peeked inside. "I have no idea. Don't these scones smell marvelous? Real Door County cherries. Charlie had a hankering for something sweet this morning so I thought I'd whip up a batch. Would you like a cup of coffee? I just made it."

"You made the coffee. And the scones." Something was wrong with this picture.

"Charlie and I were getting hungry, so I thought I better rustle up some breakfast before we go hiking."

Alex's back teeth came together. There was no sign of Kate because Kate wasn't here.

One of the guests was preparing her own breakfast. In the bed-and-*breakfast*.

"Excuse me a minute." Alex walked onto the deck and punched in Kate's number but the call went right to her voice mail.

"This is Kate. Leave a message and I'll call you back."

He shut the phone off.

"This is the day that the Lord made and it's a fine one, isn't it, Mr. Porter?" a cheerful voice boomed behind him.

Alex hadn't realized he had company. Charlie Gibson sat in one of the wicker chairs, one hand holding a steaming cup of coffee, the other resting on the Bible in his lap.

He managed a tight smile. "Good morning, Mr. Gibson."

"Charlie, remember."

"Charlie." Discreetly, Alex hit the redial button and heard the same chipper response. "Have you seen Kate this morning?"

Irene sailed over, holding a tray of scones. "Are you going to join us, Mr. Porter?"

"Irene makes the best scones in the state of Wisconsin."

His wife blushed. "He's just a wee bit prejudiced."

"I'm sorry, Mr. and Mrs. Gibson."

The couple looked at each other.

"Sorry for what, Mr. Porter?" Irene finally ventured.

"That Kate wasn't here to make your breakfast this morning."

"Oh, don't worry about that." Charlie shook open a linen napkin. "Irene loves to putter in the kitchen."

Alex searched their faces for frustration or resentment but couldn't find either. Apparently the couple didn't mind making their own breakfast.

But he did.

"Sit down, sit down," Irene clucked. "There's plenty for everyone."

"I appreciate the offer, Mrs. Gibson, but I have to track down Kate."

Charlie chuckled. "Good luck with that, son. That girl reminds me of a hummingbird—never lands in one place for very long."

And that was the trouble, Alex thought

grimly as he excused himself. The plate of steaming cherry scones was proof that she was too busy. It was the reason he'd decided to cancel the afternoon tea, to scale down some of her duties, but the flyers plastered around the grounds told him that Kate hadn't seen it that way.

"I'll wrap one up and leave it on your desk for a midmorning snack," Irene called after him.

"Thank you."

Cody Lang was pushing a battered mountain bike up the driveway when Alex rounded the corner of the main lodge.

"Hey, Mr. Porter. Where's Kate?"

"I have no idea." But he planned to find her.

Disappointment skimmed the surface of the boy's eyes. Alex remembered what Kate had said about Cody's home life and paused.

"Mrs. Gibson made a batch of scones this morning. You can have mine if you'd like."

"Thanks!" Cody abandoned the bike and sprinted toward the inn.

Five minutes later, Alex was pulling up in front of the café.

Penelope—Alex inwardly cringed that he

thought about a bicycle in terms of a name—was propped up against the side of the building.

The breakfast rush was in full swing. Missy Martin skipped from table to table and Grady's off-key whistle ricocheted around the kitchen.

Alex pushed through the swinging saloon-style doors and ran into Grady's scowl.

"Complaint cards are by the cash register," the old cook barked out.

"I'm looking for Kate."

"Then you should be looking at the bed-and-breakfast, 'cause that's where she is every morning 'bout this time. Order up!"

For the first time, Alex felt a stab of concern. He'd assumed Kate had overslept or gotten waylaid by one of many people who looked to her to fix the town's problems.

"She didn't show up this morning."

Something in Alex's expression must have registered with Grady, because he frowned. "I haven't seen her, either."

"I'll be back."

Alex took the stairs up to Kate's apartment two at a time and knocked on the door.

Just when he was about to call Jake Sutton, the knob rattled and turned.

"Kate, what—"

"Shh."

Alex's gaze dropped two feet. Through a narrow crack in the door, a boy about seven or eight years old stared up at him.

"Are you a p'liceman?"

"No—."

The door began to close again.

"Wait!" Alex managed to wedge his toe into the gap before it shut. "I'm looking for Kate. Can I come in?"

"Nope. You're a stranger."

"Not to Kate. I'm her boss." If Kate was within earshot, that statement alone would bring her running. "She didn't show up for work this morning."

Wary blue eyes studied him. Alex could have easily pushed the door open but some inner prompting warned him against it. He knelt down until he and the boy were eye level.

"I'm Alex. What's your name?"

"Logan J. Gardner."

Alex's lips edged up in a smile. "Can you let Kate know that I'm here?"

The boy shook his head and a swatch of pale, white-blond hair fell across his eyes. "She's sleepin'."

"Sleeping?" At eight-thirty? Alex tried unsuccessfully to see inside the apartment.

"But I'm hungry." Logan glanced over his shoulder. "She said we could have blueberry pancakes for breakfast this morning."

We?

"Kate doesn't like people to be hungry," Alex said slowly. "I'm sure she won't mind if we wake her up and remind her about the pancakes."

Hunger trumped the boy's initial caution.

"Okay." Logan edged away from his post.

Alex stepped inside. It took a few seconds for his eyes to adjust to the gloom. The shades were drawn over the windows. His foot caught on something and he shook it free. Looking down, Alex saw a stained backpack stamped with the face of a popular cartoon character, the contents scattered around it.

He had visited Kate's apartment and seen firsthand the meticulous condition she kept the kitchen at the inn. The disarray wasn't in keeping with the Kate he was getting to know.

"See?" Logan pointed to the sofa.

Alex's heart jumped in his chest.

Kate was sound asleep, her arms wrapped around a little girl whose wispy hair was the same shade of platinum as the boy's.

"That's Tori." Logan shuffled closer, his eyes dark with apprehension. "She likes pancakes, but she doesn't like strangers, either."

Alex didn't miss the "either" and summoned what he hoped was a reassuring smile before bending down.

Kate's cheeks were flushed with color, her breathing slow and even. The thick fringe of russet lashes clashed with the lavender shadows below her eyes.

Was she sick?

"Kate?"

A pair of eyes popped open. Blue, not green.

And then a piercing scream rent the air.

* * *

Kate sat up so quickly she almost dumped Tori onto the floor.

"It's okay, sweetie," she rasped.

The screaming intensified as Tori's thin arms locked around Kate's neck.

As Kate tried to comfort her, several things began to penetrate the fog in her brain. A sliver of sunlight—bright sunlight—edged the windowsill, which meant she'd slept through the alarm.

Wait a second, had she even *set* the alarm?

Logan, a miniature sentinel in pajamas that were two sizes too small, hovered at the end of the sofa, his gaze darting from her to...

Alex.

Suddenly, Kate wanted to dive under the blanket and scream, too.

His presence could only mean one thing. She should have been at work. Kate peeked at the clock...

Two hours ago.

But she couldn't deal with Alex at the moment, not when Tori continued to emit an earsplitting sound that rivaled a smoke detector. Any minute now, the volunteer fire department would be pounding on her door.

"Shhh." Kate gathered the little girl against her. "It's all right. I've got you. There's nothing to be afraid of."

Alex strode over to the row of windows and the shades snapped up, one at a time. Drenching the room in sunlight.

Amazingly enough, the screaming stopped.

Tori drew a long, shuddering breath and peered at Alex over Kate's shoulder.

Kate's initial relief dissolved as the sun shone like a spotlight on the fallout from the telephone call she'd received at midnight.

She'd made the kids something to eat before putting them to bed and the cleanup had had to wait while she ran a bath for Tori and found a clean T-shirt in the drawer to double as a nightgown.

Logan had trudged to the bedroom, half-asleep following a quick shower, but his sister had been so distraught, Kate had let her stay up a little longer. She'd pulled out some of her old picture books and read to Tori until she fell into an exhausted slumber.

At some point, Kate must have done the same thing.

Alex stepped in front of her and she tried not to squirm under his steady gaze.

No doubt she looked even worse than the apartment. She'd fallen asleep wearing the sweatpants and T-shirt she'd thrown on when Jake Sutton and Grace Eversea had shown up at her door. Her curls sprang out from her head like rusty bedsprings and she was pretty sure the button on the sofa pillow had left a permanent indentation in her cheek.

Why, God? Why does Alex always have to see me looking like...me?

"Logan said you promised to make blueberry pancakes." The quiet timbre of Alex's voice swept the rest of the cobwebs away.

"That's right." Kate scraped a smile for Logan's sake, even as guilt poked at her.

What had Irene and Charlie and the rest of the guests done for breakfast in her absence?

"Would you like some pancakes, too, sweetheart?" she murmured in Tori's ear.

The blond head bobbed once.

"Great." Kate pushed to her feet, Tori still clinging to her.

Alex took a step forward and the anger banked in his eyes made her flinch.

"I have to get back to the inn," he said tightly.

Kate tried to straighten her shoulders but found it difficult with Tori attached to her like a barnacle.

"I'll be there in an hour," she promised.

His chin dipped. "Fine. I'll see you then."

Oh, he'd see her—but Kate had serious doubts that everything would be fine.

Chapter Fourteen

❦

"There's the lake."

For the first time, Kate saw a flicker of interest in Logan's eyes, quickly extinguished when Tori whimpered and buried her face in her blanket. He patted her shoulder and whispered something in her ear that brought out a tremulous smile again.

It was heartbreaking, the way the boy looked out for his younger sibling.

While he and Tori had devoured a platter of blueberry pancakes and sausage, Kate had straightened up the apartment. As the sixty-minute countdown ticked by, she'd sacrificed her morning shower to throw a load of the children's laundry in the washing machine. It had also taken her a few precious minutes to coax Lucy and Ethel out from under the bed. The cats had taken cover under Kate's bed when Tori started screaming and only a can of tuna had convinced them that all was right with the world once more.

Even though Thor's engine had fired up, they were still pulling into the driveway fifteen minutes late.

Kate's heart sank when she saw an unfamiliar SUV parked next to one of the cabins. While she'd been sleeping, more of the guests had arrived.

She unbuckled Tori from the booster seat Grace had supplied and anchored her against one hip.

"That guy's fishing." Logan spotted to a portly figure standing on the end of the dock.

Charlie Gibson lifted his arm in a friendly wave.

"We can walk down there and see if he caught anything in a little while," Kate promised.

If Alex didn't banish her from the property.

Logan stuck close as they walked up the cobblestone path to the front door. Kate noticed that he never ventured far from his little sister.

Lady and Mulligan streaked toward them and Tori froze.

"They won't hurt you." Kate stopped to pet the dogs but Tori melted against her and even Logan shied away from the dogs' attention.

There was no sign of Alex so she took a short detour on her way to the kitchen. Unlike most bed-and-breakfasts that catered to adults, Abby's inn was family-friendly. Kate found several puzzles stashed away in an antique trunk in the gathering room and brought them to the kitchen.

Thankfully, Tori didn't protest as Kate gently deposited her on a chair at the table.

She poured two glasses of milk and set out a plate of cinnamon rolls.

"Do you see that door across the hall? That's where I'll be and you can call if you need me, okay?"

The siblings remained silent, as if they were used to being left to fend for themselves.

Kate pulled in a breath and released it slowly but her pulse kept jumping like a pogo stick. The office door was open so she didn't bother knocking.

Not when Alex was expecting her.

He turned from the window, his expression remote. "Irene Gibson made scones this morning."

Kate latched onto the back of a chair as a wave of fatigue crashed over her.

Something flickered in his eyes. "Do you want to tell me what happened?"

Would it do any good? Kate wanted to ask. But there was no getting around the fact that she had dropped the ball that morning, the very thing Alex had warned her would happen.

Kate licked her lips. "My friend, Grace Eversea, called around midnight. She had an emergency."

"So you agreed to babysit," Alex guessed. "Knowing you had to be here at five to make breakfast."

"Grace isn't just a friend, she's a social worker." Kate expelled a ragged breath. "And I'm not babysitting. I'm...licensed for emergency foster care. Tori and Logan didn't have anywhere else to go so she brought them to me."

* * *

Foster care.

The two words—and all the implications—hit Alex with the force of a front line wind.

He'd assumed that Kate had blown off her responsibilities at the inn because she couldn't tell people "no."

He'd also assumed she would be alone when she came back.

"But you're single."

"Single people can become foster parents." Kate sank into the chair she'd been clinging to. "Grace and I went to high school together. A few years ago, she mentioned there was a shortage of foster care parents in the county. I agreed to take in kids on a short-term emergency basis. It was all I could do, because of the café. I haven't had anyone for a long time, but last night Grace called and…" Her voice trailed off, leaving him to fill in the blank.

And Kate couldn't say no.

"How long will they be staying with you?"

"I'm not sure. Their mother is addicted to pain pills. Yesterday, she left a cigarette burning while she was passed out and almost burned the house down.

"Grace said that she agreed to check herself into an inpatient treatment center, but she's been estranged from her family for years and the children's father has never been part of their lives. Right now, DHS is trying to locate an aunt to find out if she'll agree to take care of them."

"That could take a while."

Kate didn't answer.

Alex sat down in the chair across from her and leaned forward.

"So, what you're telling me," he said softly, "is that you plan to run the café, work here part-time and take care of two traumatized children."

Kate leaned forward, too, and a glimmer of humor cut through the weariness.

"See, I knew there was more to you than just a pretty face," she said.

Kate couldn't believe she had had the audacity to tease him. She was punchy from lack of sleep, that was the only explanation.

For a moment, it looked as if Alex were battling a smile. Did sleep deprivation cause hallucinations?

"Do you know how difficult it's going to be to haul those two children back and forth every day?"

Leave it to Alex to zero in on her number one concern.

"Yes."

"And your apartment is…small."

That was number two.

"If I had to make a guess, I'd say Tori and Logan are going to need a lot of attention, considering what they've been through recently."

Yup, that was the third one. But acknowledging those things didn't outweigh the truth. Tori and Logan needed her. But more importantly, they needed to stay together and Grace had brought them to her door because Kate had been the only one willing to take both of them.

A small part of her had hoped that Alex would understand. That he would feel sorry for two kids who'd gone through a traumatic experience and needed someone to care about them.

But with Alex Porter, it was all about business.

If he hired someone else to take her place

for the remainder of the two weeks, Concern Number One would disappear. But Kate didn't want to let Abby down.

Should she call her friend and explain the situation? No, that would seem too much like tattling. Maybe Alex was right. Maybe in this instance, she *had* taken on more than she could handle.

"Kate—"

A crash came from the direction of the kitchen, followed by a wail that brought both of them to their feet.

Kate sprinted past Alex and skidded through an expanding puddle of liquid on the floor. Tori was cowering under the table and Logan, his face as white as the milk pooling at his feet, had positioned himself between his sister and the adults who had responded to the commotion.

"She didn't mean to do it!" Logan had to pitch his voice above Tori's muffled sobs.

Alex grabbed a roll of paper towel as Kate knelt down in front of the boy.

"It's not your fault, Logan. Accidents happen."

For all his apparent bravery, Logan's lower lip trembled. "We didn't want to bother you."

Kate sized up the situation immediately and understood. Even though she'd encouraged the children to let her know if they needed anything, they hadn't believed her.

She rocked back on her heels. "Tori," she coaxed softly. "Come out from under the table and I'll pour you some more milk."

Tears continued to stream down the pudgy cheeks. "Is there more?" she whispered.

Out of the corner of her eye, Kate saw Alex stiffen.

Hiding her emotions, she put out her hand. "There's more."

The girl regarded her warily and then flicked an uncertain look at her older brother.

Logan nodded and Tori crawled out from under the table, dragging her ragged blanket.

Kate resisted the urge to sweep Tori into her arms and hug the stuffing out of her.

Give me wisdom, Lord. This kids have been through so much. I pray they will begin to trust me...and learn to trust You.

In the midst of the silent prayer, Kate remembered that none of this had taken God by surprise. Tori and Logan had been placed in her care for a reason and God would give her the strength she needed to handle it.

He always did.

She turned toward the refrigerator to retrieve the gallon of milk, but Alex had beat her to it.

"Here you go."

Kate's throat swelled as Alex set another glass of milk on the table.

"Thank you," she murmured.

He inclined his head, his expression shuttered.

Kate could only imagine what he was thinking. If a simple accident like a glass of spilled milk wrenched a reaction like this from the five-year-old, what would trigger the next one? And where would they be when it occurred?

"We can finish our conversation in the hall," Kate said, reluctant to leave the children again.

Besides that, how long could it take for Alex to say "This isn't going to work"?

They stepped out of the kitchen and Kate braced herself.

"As far as I can see, there's only one solution," Alex said without preamble.

He was going to hire someone to take her place...

"The three of you will have to stay here."

"Here?"

Kate's eyes widened, as if she wasn't sure she'd heard him correctly.

But, yes, Alex realized he had said the words out loud.

"Abby's suite on the third floor has two bedrooms, a private bath and a living room," Alex pointed out.

Kate's brow furrowed. "Isn't that where you're staying?"

"Abby hasn't opened up any of the rooms in the lodge for guests yet, so I can move into one on the second floor."

Kate didn't look surprised by the admission and Alex realized that, at some point, his sister had shared the details of her past.

Although Abby had come a long way from the shy young woman uncomfortable in social situations, she had decided that it would be best if she rented out the cabins and lived in the main lodge alone until Quinn moved in with her after the honeymoon.

Abby had confided that she wasn't where she wanted to be as far as trusting people, but opening the rooms in the inn was a step in the right direction.

Over Kate's shoulder, Alex saw Logan awkwardly pat his little sister's shoulder and felt an unexpected tightening in his chest.

Logan's protective stance reminded him of another boy who had been given the responsibility of protecting his little sister. Tori was close to the age Abby had been when she'd been abducted and he recognized some of the same symptoms of emotional trauma. Not only in the tears and emotional outbursts, but in the mixture of confusion and betrayal that clouded the innocence in her eyes.

"Aren't you worried they'll disturb the guests?"

Kate's question tugged Alex back to the present.

Was she *trying* to change his mind?

"The only thing that might disturb the guests is having to eat Irene Gibson's scones again," he countered. "If you stay at the lodge, you won't have to wake Tori and Logan up at five in the morning. And you'll be able keep an eye on them out the kitchen window if they want to play outside."

Kate didn't look convinced. "Won't they disturb *you?*"

"Probably," Alex admitted. "But I'm getting used to being disturbed." He gave her a meaningful look; but, for once, Kate didn't rise to the bait.

"It would be nice if they had some more space," she said slowly.

"I'll have my things moved out of Abby's rooms by the time you come back this afternoon."

Kate stared up at him, a dazed look on her face. "I can't believe it. You're supposed to talk me out of this. Tell me that I'm crazy."

Alex was beginning to think that word described *him*.

Kate had no boundaries. Everyone, it seemed, was given access to her life.

Alex *should* be telling her that it wasn't smart. It wasn't even safe. But then an image of Kate, her arms wrapped protectively around Tori, had flashed through his mind. And made Alex want to protect *her*.

Something he didn't want to analyze too closely.

"I doubt I could talk you out of it," Alex said. "And just for the record, I do think you're crazy."

Kate smiled.

"You do realize that you're giving up the perfect opportunity to fire me?"

Yes, he did.

Alex didn't want to analyze that too closely, either.

Chapter Fifteen

Kate tucked a lightweight blanket over Tori's shoulders and backed out of the room. After a morning of chasing Mulligan and Lady through the garden, followed by a lesson in wrapping silverware from Missy at the café, the little girl had barely been able to keep her eyes open while Kate read a chapter out of *The Secret Garden*.

Downstairs, she heard the opening notes of one of Beethoven's sonatas in the gathering room. Zoey must have arrived to practice before the afternoon tea officially began.

Ducking into her bedroom, Kate replaced her jeans shorts, T-shirt and flip-flops for a plaid sundress and dainty flats.

Abby had warned her that while most activities at the inn were the informal, "come as you are" type, she had discovered that women embraced the idea of a traditional high tea and came dressed for the part.

Pausing in front of the mirror, Kate tugged a straw cloche over her curls. A touch of mascara, a swipe of ginger-colored lip gloss and she was ready to greet the guests.

From her vantage point on the third floor, Kate spotted Logan playing with Zach and Tim Davis at the edge of the water. The teenagers, brothers who attended the youth group at Church of the Pines, had offered to take the boy under their wing for the day.

After checking on Tori one more time, she bounded down the stairs and met Emma coming out of the kitchen. Her friend had also dressed for the occasion in a filmy lavender dress, strappy sandals and a strand of matched pearls.

"Did Tori finally fall asleep?"

Kate nodded. "I think she'll be out for the rest of the afternoon."

"The tables are all set and I put the centerpieces out." Emma linked her arm through

Kate's as they walked toward the gathering room. "What else would you like me to do?"

"Pray."

Emma laughed. "I haven't stopped doing that since you called yesterday and told me about Logan and Tori."

"Tori had a rough night," Kate said in a low voice. "She woke up a lot, crying and calling out for her mother."

Kate was sure that Alex would have heard the commotion, but he hadn't said a word about it at breakfast that morning.

Tori had warmed up to her surroundings as the day progressed, smiling as she watched the dogs romp in the yard and even helping Kate with the tea preparations by dipping violets into superfine sugar to decorate the tops of the petit fours.

"What about Logan?"

"Adjusting a little better than his sister," Kate told her. "Tim and Zach have been great with him today. The three of them helped Jeremy and Cody with the tree fort and now they're catching crayfish."

Emma gave her a knowing look. "And Alex?"

"I'm not sure. He was busy checking in the new guests and over the past few hours he's been holed up in his office."

But then again, maybe there was her answer!

True to his word, though, Alex had brought Kate and the children up to Abby's suite of rooms when they returned to the inn after lunch.

"There's a bed," Kate had heard Logan whisper to his sister, breaking her heart all over again.

What sort of environment had the children called home?

Kate had seen Alex's lips tighten and wondered if he'd been thinking the same thing. Or maybe he was having second thoughts about inviting two bedraggled kids and their equally bedraggled foster mother into his well-ordered life.

"He probably took refuge in his office to avoid all the ladies in hats." Emma chuckled. "Most men—including Jake—sure would!"

Zoey switched from the soothing classical piece to a lively folk tune when they entered the room. After finishing the song, she rose to her feet and dipped an exaggerated curtsy.

Kate and Emma clapped their hands and Zoey grinned.

"I think that song goes well with tea and crumpets, don't you?"

Kate grinned back, feeling some of the tension in her shoulders ease.

The next half-hour before the guests arrived left little time for conversation. Kate zipped back and forth between the sitting room and the kitchen with trays of dainty sandwiches and bite-size desserts while Emma brewed the tea.

Zoey continued to play quietly in the background as the women began to file into the room and search the tables for their individual place settings.

After serving each table, Kate dashed upstairs to check on Tori while the women settled in.

She peeked through the crack in the door. Tori was sound asleep, one hand clutching the blanket as if it were the one familiar thing that she could hold on to.

Kate wanted to keep her forever even

though she knew it was only a matter of time before the children were either placed in a permanent foster home or with a family member.

Grace had called earlier in the afternoon with an update. She had traced an old address and discovered that the children's aunt, a Jenna Gardner, resided in the Twin Cities but so far she hadn't been able to get in touch with her.

Kate secretly had her doubts that an estranged relative would be willing to put her life on hold to care for two young children, but she had been praying that whoever this woman was, she would make room in her life—and her heart—for them.

"What's all the noise I hear in the background? I thought people checked into a bed-and-breakfast to get away from it all."

So had Alex, who mentally cuffed himself on the back of the head for not ignoring the phone when Jeff Gaines' number had appeared on the screen. Once he told the truth, Alex knew he would never live it down. Fortunately, Jeff's visits to Chicago were limited to once or twice a year, when they fought for domination on the racquetball court.

"Abby hosts a weekly tea party for her guests."

"A tea party?"

"That's what I said," Alex growled. "So, what's going on with you?"

"Not so fast." Laughter flowed beneath the words. "Your day sounds much more interesting than mine. I want details."

"Earl Gray. China cups. Fussy little cakes. Cucumber sandwiches." A vegetable that, in Alex's opinion, didn't belong between two slices of bread. "And hats."

Lots of hats.

"I can't imagine you presiding over a tea party." But the amusement in Jeff's voice told Alex that he was trying.

"I'm not." Alex's back teeth snapped together. "Kate is."

"Kate Nichols?"

"That's right."

"I didn't realize you two knew each other," Jeff said carefully.

Too carefully.

Alex scowled into the phone.

Do you know Kate? he was tempted to ask. The White Wolf Run condos were located half an hour north of Mirror Lake; but it was possible Jeff and Kate's paths crossed occasionally.

"She's doing the food prep here," he said. "Splitting her time between the inn and the café while Abby and Quinn are on their honeymoon."

"That sounds like Kate." The admiration in Jeff's voice was unmistakable now. "She's pretty energetic."

"Energetic?" Alex supposed that was one way of putting it. "If she wasn't tied down by the café, she could be running Porter Lakeside." Or at least the city of Chicago.

"So hire her."

"I tried," Alex retorted.

"You actually offered her a *job?*" Jeff said slowly.

Alex hesitated. He'd been teasing Kate that day.

Hadn't he?

"She won't leave Mirror Lake."

"I have to admit, the place does grow on a person," his friend allowed.

"And holds them here." Holds them back. "Kate's talents are wasted in a town like this. If she had time to venture past the city limits, she'd realize it, too."

"Wow." A low whistle pierced Alex's eardrum. "I never thought I'd see the day that Alex Porter would have such strong feelings."

"We lived in the same frat house," Alex reminded him. "You saw a lot of those days."

"Not your feelings about Kate staying in Mirror Lake. Your feelings about *Kate*."

"Feelings?"

"Feelings." Jeff stretched the word into at least four syllables. "Do I have to spell the word for you? Or just spell it out?"

"Don't be ridiculous," Alex snapped. "We argue all the time."

They even argued about the fact they weren't arguing.

Alex remembered their phone conversation and smiled.

"Uh-huh," Jeff said smugly, as if he'd *seen* the smile.

Alex opened his mouth to tell Jeff he should spend more time at the gym and less time on the couch watching daytime talk shows when he saw a furtive movement outside the door.

"Sorry to cut this short, but I have to deal with something."

"Yes, you do. And I'd apologize, but someone had to point out that are you *are* human and it's perfectly natural to have—"

"Something else, Jeff." Alex rolled his eyes and hung up the phone.

A flutter of pink told him that Tori was still lingering outside the door.

The hum of conversation, punctuated by outbursts of laughter in the gathering room, must have been the reason she hadn't flown directly to Kate's side when she woke up from her nap.

Alex hesitated as he reached for the doorknob; his ears were still ringing from the last time he'd inadvertently startled the kid.

"Knock, knock," he said, taking a risk that Tori loved the silliness of the jokes the way Abby had at that age.

Alex had spent hours making up new ones in those first few days after the police had brought her home. It had been the only way he could get his sister to talk to him.

"Who's there?" a voice whispered on the other side of the door.

"Butter."

"B-butter who?"

"Butter open the door and see for yourself."

A muffled giggle followed and then the door slid open another inch. Wide, periwinkle-blue eyes studied Alex over the top of the book cradled in her arms.

He glanced at the clock on the wall. The afternoon tea Kate had insisted on going ahead with was proving to be a success. Such a success that the guests seemed to be in no hurry to leave.

"Should we find your brother?" The last time Alex had seen Logan, he'd been splashing around in the shallow water with two teenage boys from the church youth group.

Tori shook her head.

Okaaay.

"Hungry?" Maybe if Kate found them in the kitchen foraging for food, she would take over and Alex could get back to work.

Tori's lower lip drooped at the corners, a sure sign he wasn't getting this right.

"What *do* you want?" Alex asked cautiously, even though he guessed what the answer would be.

Sure enough, she pressed the book more tightly against her middle and glanced toward the entrance of the gathering room.

"Kate can't read to you right now. She's busy with the tea." The tea that would have been canceled, if Alex had had his way.

Tears splashed over the breaker of golden lashes.

And Alex caved in.

"What page are you on?"

"Do you think they're planning to stay until breakfast tomorrow morning?" Emma whispered as Kate hastily replenished the dessert tray for the third time.

"I'm beginning to wonder that myself." The event was only scheduled to last an hour and a half, but the guests were having so much fun they continued to linger, long after the last cucumber sandwich had been reduced to crumbs.

"You could always serve s'mores if we run out of food," Emma teased.

"Those are for the campfire this evening."

Kate blew a curl off her forehead and handed her friend the tray. "Can you take these out? I'm going to run upstairs and check on Tori again. I know she was tired, but she's been asleep for over an hour."

Emma smiled. "She's awake."

"Awake?" Kate repeated the word. "When? Where is she? Did she go outside?"

"Take it easy, Mom." Amusement danced in Emma's eyes. "She's in the three-seasons room. I peeked in on her a few minutes ago and trust me, she's in good hands."

Tim and Zach.

Kate breathed a sigh of relief. For going above and beyond the call of duty, she was going to make the teens a batch of the triple chocolate brownies they loved.

She made her way to the spacious glassed-in room off the library, one of several additions the camp's previous owners had tacked on to the main lodge over the years. Steeped in sunlight and crowded with plants and the comfortable furnishings Abby favored, it offered a quiet refuge...

Kate braked in the doorway when she spotted a familiar pair of Italian leather shoes propped up on the low wicker table.

Alex didn't *nap* during the day. Unless the anguished cries of a five-year-old who missed her mother had kept him awake half the night. Or he'd sought a quiet place to escape the gaggle of women who'd invaded the inn at *her* invitation.

Either way, Kate knew she was somehow to blame.

She started to back away—quietly—when a blond head popped up in the chair next to Alex. A bright smile lit up the small, heart-shaped face.

"Me an' Alex are readin' the book. See?"

Kate sagged against the doorframe.

Did she see?

Yes.

Would she have believed it if she hadn't spotted Tori resting in the crook of Alex's arm, holding up Kate's ancient copy of *The Secret Garden* as evidence?

Not in a million years.

Chapter Sixteen

"It's a beautiful night, isn't it?"

The French doors slid open with a whisper behind Alex, and he stiffened.

"You're still awake." He hadn't meant to sound so accusing, but Kate had escorted the children upstairs over an hour ago and Alex assumed she'd turned in for the night, too.

"I had a few things to take care of."

That didn't surprise Alex. Kate always had something—or someone—to take care of.

She came to stand beside him on the deck, a cup of coffee cradled in her palms and a smile on her face. "I whipped up a few pans of stuffed French toast for the guests for breakfast tomorrow morning."

Alex's gaze skimmed Kate's slender frame. For the campfire, she'd worn figure-hugging jeans and a faded green hoodie to provide insulation against the mosquitoes. At some point, and he had no idea when, she'd switched to black sweatpants, a T-shirt dotted with winged cupcakes and an apron knotted around her waist.

"So you ducked into a nearby phone booth?"

"I don't follow."

"Orders?" Alex muttered.

Kate grinned. "No, I mean, you have to spell it out. It's after ten and this is decaf."

Feelings...do I have to spell the word or spell it out for you?

Jeff Gaines's laughing comment rudely intruded on Alex's thoughts.

He politely but firmly kicked it aside.

"I mean you've changed clothes three times today for three different events. Maybe you should just throw on a cape like all the other superheroes and save time."

"A cape." The clover-green eyes brightened, as if the idea appealed to her.

"You're completely missing the point."

"You can't serve tea and scones in blue jeans and you can't serve s'mores in a fancy dress."

"That's just it. You didn't have to supervise the campfire this evening. Or lead the sing-along. Or make sure the pieces of chocolate remained in direct proportion to the number of graham crackers."

Kate tilted her head to look at him. A band of moonlight slid across her face, caressing her jaw and weaving strands of silver into the copper curls.

"And *you* didn't have to keep an eye on Tori this afternoon."

Alex had hoped she wouldn't bring that up.

"I didn't think Tori would like tea." And Alex didn't like tears, so reading a book had risen to the top of his "to do" list.

Until Kate had found them.

He would have turned the book over to her immediately, but Tori had insisted that he finish reading the page.

Kate perched in the chair across from them, a half smile on her face. It had taken all of Alex's self-control to keep his eyes fixed on the printed words and not on the shapely, sun-kissed legs visible below the hem of her sundress.

He'd retreated to his office as quickly as possible and hadn't caught more than a few glimpses of them as the evening wore on. Logan and Tori stayed close to Kate while she'd started the campfire and welcomed the guests who, Alex suspected, were as drawn to Kate's laughter as they were to the promise of something sweet.

Alex had spent the past few hours on the phone with his attorney, who'd called him after being approached with another you-can't-refuse-this offer from a major hotel chain that been trying to buy him out for years.

He'd refused it, but not quite as enthusiastically as he had in the past. Something Alex couldn't quite explain. Not to his attorney or to himself.

"Tori wanted me to tell you good night. And that she likes your peanut-butter sandwiches the best because you cut the crusts off." Kate looked at him curiously. "How did you know that, by the way?"

Alex shrugged. "I've had a lot of experience with books and tea parties. When they get older, it changes to movies and pizza."

"Well, I think you made a new friend. Don't be surprised if she wants you to read chapter three."

"As long as it's not in the middle of the night."

"You heard her." The words rolled out on a sigh. "Tori fights to stay awake. It's like she's afraid to close her eyes."

"Leave a light on," Alex suggested. "She probably doesn't like the dark."

Kate's brow puckered. "I didn't think about that."

Alex had.

"She reminds me of Abby at that age," he said without thinking. And immediately regretted the words. It was something Alex didn't talk about. A part of the past he didn't want to *think* about.

"What happened to Abby...it must have been devastating for you and your parents."

The quiet acknowledgment stripped the air from Alex's lungs. Even the people who remembered what had happened knew not to bring it up.

"She told you." Alex had had his suspicions, but the compassion reflected in Kate's eyes confirmed them.

"We're friends," she said simply. "She told me that as a child she'd been abducted by one of the hotel employees."

"Did she mention that he was also a family friend?" Alex's hands tightened on the rail.

"Yes." Kate handed him the coffee cup, an unspoken invitation to share.

After a moment's hesitation, Alex took it from her. The intimacy of the gesture and the connection it created between them nudged him off balance.

Alex wasn't sure what Abby had told Kate, but suddenly he wanted her to see it through *his* eyes. And he wanted her to understand why it was dangerous to trust. To give people access to your life.

"Porter Lakeside was our parents' first hotel and they worked round the clock, right alongside the staff, pitching in wherever someone needed help.

"I remember pushing Abby down the halls in a laundry cart and sneaking down to the kitchen in my pajamas to have a piece of cake. Even when our parents bought another hotel and started to get reviewed in travel magazines, it felt as if everyone was one big, happy family. Until one of the employees was caught stealing and Dad had to fire him. Abby didn't know that when Carl asked her to get in his car. She trusted him."

Alex had trusted him, too.

"Abby said your parents had you change schools."

"Not just schools." *Everything.* "We moved to an estate outside the city with more gates and security cameras than the art museum. Mom and Dad didn't socialize with the staff anymore and we weren't allowed to, either."

"That must have been really hard," Kate said softly.

"No." Not for him, anyway. "Dad explained it was up to him and I, as the men of the family, to make sure nothing like that ever happened again."

"But you were only fourteen…he made you promise to look out for Abby?"

"I made a promise to myself." Alex's jaw tightened. "After I inherited the hotels, I decided to run things the same way my parents did. It works."

* * *

Who are you trying to convince? Kate wanted to ask. *Me? Or yourself?*

She'd been stunned when she had found him reading to Tori in the three-seasons room. Her assumption that Alex didn't care for children had shattered when she watched the little girl tuck her cheek against the broad shoulder and saw the remains of a tea party on the table.

"I've had a lot of experience with books and tea parties. When they get older, it changes to movies and pizza."

Kate wondered if he realized what he'd revealed.

Alex knew what he was doing because he'd done it before.

At the age of fourteen, he been charged with the responsibility of protecting his sister after the unthinkable happened. At twenty-two, he'd taken on the added weight of protecting his parents' dream. And sacrificed his own in the process.

It was easy to focus on the cynical executive Alex had become and forget that he'd once navigated his younger sister through the turbulent teens.

Fragments of conversations Kate had had with Abby fell into place like pieces of a puzzle.

To cope with two life-altering events that would have shaken anyone to the core, Alex had chosen to order his life in a certain way.

The Grand Plan.

Not a goal to become a household name or amass a fortune but to live in such a way that he maintained control. Not only over himself, but everything around him.

Every*one* around him.

"Matt Wilde left a message for you about the picnic tomorrow." Alex slanted a look at her. "On my phone."

Kate recognized the comment for what it was, a not-so-subtle attempt to change the topic. Maybe Alex already regretted revisiting a painful part of his past. She wanted to know more but knew he wasn't a man who allowed any weakness to show.

Something had just happened. A subtle shift in their relationship that left her feeling both hopeful...and terrified.

"And you didn't call him back and cancel that, too?" Kate strove to keep her tone light.

"I would have, if I thought it would do any good." Alex pushed the cup toward her. "But I arranged for the college students Abby hired to clean the cabins to come back tomorrow evening so you wouldn't have the extra cleanup."

"I don't know." Kate looked thoughtful. "Asking the housekeeping crew to clean up the kitchen would fall under my duties, wouldn't it?"

"I mentioned it when they stopped by *my* office."

"I don't think that counts."

Alex shrugged. "I'm the boss and I say it does."

"Temporary boss." Kate began to inch away from the rail.

He pretended to consider that. Rejected it with a shake of his head. "No, I still heard the word 'boss' in there."

"Fine. But that means that I can play by those rules, too. If you can add to an employee's hours in your office, I can use the phone in *my* kitchen to cut them." Kate shot toward the sliding glass doors to make that call but Alex had already anticipated the move.

Halfway across the deck, a strong arm snagged her around the waist. Kate felt herself being lifted off her feet and turned around.

"Rats," she breathed. "I forgot you're a runner."

Alex didn't release her and for some reason, it didn't occur to Kate to try to escape.

Exasperation deepened his eyes to evergreen. "Are you always this contrary?"

Kate thought about that.

"No," she said honestly. "I don't think so. Do you always chase down your employees when you don't get your way?"

Alex thought about that.

"No. I don't think so."

"See, if you were really my boss, I wouldn't last a week." Why had she brought *that* up?

"That's true." That slow, rare smile kicked up the corners of Alex's lips and sent Kate's heart into a freefall. "You'd set a terrible example for the rest of my minions."

"I should—" *escape!* "—Go inside."

"Planning to rescue that last piece of chocolate cake before the evil genius gets his hands on it?"

"Evil genius?"

"You play your part and I'll play mine," Alex deadpanned.

No fair. He was being charming again.

Laughter backlit his eyes and Kate caught a fascinating glimpse of the young man who'd loved to play practical jokes on his friends. The older brother who had sent his sister careening through the hotel corridors in a laundry cart.

The man who had patiently tweaked the blueprints for a tree fort and took an hour out of his busy day to read to a five-year-old.

A man it would be all too easy to fall in love with.

To break the power of that smile and the effect it was having on her, Kate took a step back but realized that Alex was holding her loosely by the wrists.

"Abby taught me some self-defense moves. Don't make me use them."

The laughter faded as Alex looked down at her and what shimmered in its place made her suck in a breath.

Kate's mind fogged up, reducing visibility to the pair of jade-green eyes staring into hers.

He was thinking about kissing her.

He was *going* to kiss her.

"Good night, Kate."

Alex let her go.

That was just as well, because if one of Alex Porter's smiles had the power to melt her defenses like sunlight on a patch of snow, Kate could only imagine what one of his kisses would do.

Alex waited until he heard Kate moving around in the kitchen before he went back inside.

Call it cowardice...or self-preservation.

When he walked into the office, the first thing he saw was the piece of chocolate cake on his desk.

Abby's desk, Alex silently corrected.

His desk, on the top floor of Porter Lakeside, was twice the size of this one and faced a trio of oval, leaded glass windows that overlooked Lake Michigan.

What was happening to him?

In a week he would be back in Chicago, where he belonged.

Alex yanked open a drawer and a piece of pink paper drifted to the floor, as if it had been waiting for just the right moment.

He picked it up and scanned the contents.

"Unless the Lord builds the house, its builders labor in vain. Unless the Lord watches over the city, the watchmen stand guard in vain."

Two things at the top of Alex's list. To build on and to protect the Porter legacy.

So why didn't they seem to be enough anymore?

There had been a time in Alex's life when he had prayed, asked God for direction, but the answers hadn't always come quickly enough to suit him. Or didn't, if he were completely honest, line up with what *he* wanted.

When the county deputy had knocked on the door in the middle of the night, Alex had come to the conclusion that maybe God didn't always listen. Or pay attention. So he had come to the conclusion that he should just take control of his life and not bother Him anymore.

Alex read the verse again, felt the words seep into cracks he had tried to patch himself over the years.

Are You trying to tell me something, Lord?

The question formed in Alex's heart and took wing before he recognized it for what it was.

A prayer.

Chapter Seventeen

Kate tiptoed past the bedroom where Tori and Logan were sleeping and made her way down to the kitchen.

Several of the guests had requested a continental breakfast delivered to their cabins, the others preferred to eat in the dining room before they checked out.

Fatigue tugged at Kate's eyelids as she started the coffee brewing and pulled a bowl of fresh fruit out of the fridge.

Thanks to Alex, she'd tossed and turned most of the night.

He'd almost kissed her.

Kissed. Her.

Kate still wasn't quite sure what had happened. One second they'd been caught up in a verbal sparring match and the next…

"It's that smile," she said under her breath.

It got to her every time.

And probably a whole lot of other women, too, Kate thought. Alex would have no trouble finding a date to watch paint dry. He was handsome, intelligent, sophisticated and totally out of her league.

She would avoid him, that's what she would do. It shouldn't be all that difficult. After the guests checked out and Matt's mentoring group invaded the grounds, Alex would close himself up in his office and do what millionaire executives did all day.

She probably wouldn't even see him…

"Cabin two requested an early checkout."

Kate almost dropped Abby's antique bowl and sent fresh berries scattering like marbles at the sound of Alex's voice.

Keeping her back to him, she plucked a knife from the butcher block and began to cut up a bunch of bananas. "The Morrows. I'll deliver their breakfast first."

"They've got a family reunion in Ashland this afternoon." Alex's tone was brisk.

Businesslike. As if he hadn't shared a cup of coffee—and a glimpse of his heart—with her the night before.

Fine, she could do that, too.

She could turn around and face Alex without remembering the warm strength of his arms. The way she'd felt when for a few moments, his smile, and his arms, had held her captive...

Or maybe not.

Kate had always prided herself on being good with relationships. She was a loyal friend. A devoted daughter. A fair boss. An encouraging mentor.

But she had no frame of reference for *this*. No idea what to do with her conflicted feelings for Alex Porter.

"Help yourself to coffee," she blurted out, still unable to look at him as she retrieved a muffin tin from the lower cabinet. "I'm serving breakfast in the dining room in an hour."

"Did someone say the word breakfast?"

Kate could have cried with relief. "Matt! I wasn't expecting you this early." *Thank you, thank you, for showing up this early!*

Her pastor sauntered into the kitchen, a

clipboard tucked under one arm and a football under the other. "I have to set up a few things before the picnic." He glanced at Alex. "I appreciate you letting the mentoring ministry use the grounds this afternoon."

"Don't thank me, thank my sister."

Matt didn't seem put off by the cool response. "The boys can get pretty rambunctious, but I promise we'll try and leave things in one piece."

"Coffee, Matt?"

"Sounds good. Thanks."

Kate's hands shook as she pulled an oversize coffee mug in the cupboard, grateful that God had provided a temporary six foot tall buffer, in the form of her pastor, between her and Alex.

She filled the cup and handed it to Matt. Steaming liquid sloshed over the rim and he looked at her in astonishment.

"I think that's the first time in two years that I've seen you spill a drop of coffee," Matt teased. "Something on your mind?"

"No. There's no one…*nothing*…at all." Kate felt the heat travel up her neck and light up every freckle on her nose.

Matt continued to study her. "Zoey told me a little about the situation with Tori and Logan. They're welcome to join us in some of the activities today."

Kate heard Alex's foot tap against the ceramic tile. If they could only bore him a little longer...

"I was going to ask you if that would be all right. The picnic was all Jeremy and Cody could talk about yesterday. They got Logan excited about meeting Dev McGuire."

A frown creased Matt's forehead. "Unfortunately, McGuire canceled at the last minute."

"Oh, no. Did he say why?"

"He left a voice mail saying that something came up and he can't make it." Some of Matt's frustration leached into his voice. "I'm not sure what to do on such short notice. The Redstones are out of town today or I'm sure Daniel would give a presentation on Native American artifacts."

Knowing how disappointed the boys would be, Kate tried to think of a replacement. "What about Ben Keller? He's one of the best fishing guides in the county. I'm sure he's got some great stories he could share with the boys."

"Ben would have been great, but he had a mild stroke about a month ago."

"I didn't know that." Kate made a mental note to add the man's name to the list of people she prayed for. "I suppose you could read a chapter out of Abby's book, 'How to Survive and Thrive in the Woods'. I saw it on the nightstand in her room."

Matt smiled. "I'm not worried. I know from experience that this kind of stuff never takes God by surprise. He has a plan."

Kate believed that, too. But she had no idea how—or even if—the man sitting at the kitchen table fit into God's plan for her.

But you want him to.

"Kate?" Matt was frowning at her. "Are you sure you're okay?"

Out of the corner of her eye, she saw Alex lean forward, as if he were waiting for the answer, too.

"Just a little preoccupied." Kate began to fill the baskets on the counter with the speed of a seasoned assembly line worker. "I have to deliver these to the cabins but help yourselves to more coffee. I'll be back in a few minutes."

As soon as the coast was clear and Alex was gone.

Before either of the men could protest—or heaven forbid, follow her—Kate dashed out the door.

The truth followed her. She could try and avoid Alex for the rest of the day, but it wouldn't matter.

He'd already worked his way into her heart.

She wasn't in danger of falling in love with Alex Porter. It had already happened.

Kate was up to her elbows in coleslaw when she heard someone tap on the screen door.

"Come on in." Everyone else was. Between guests checking out and boys arriving for the mentoring picnic, the inn had been Grand Central Station all morning.

It hadn't taken long for the adult mentors to coax Logan into joining the fun and the boys didn't seem to mind that Tori tagged along, giving Kate an opportunity to get the fixings ready for the evening cookout.

"Hey, Kate."

A large, Doug-shaped shadow fell over her workspace.

"Hi." Kate returned the greeting cautiously. "What are you doing here? It's Saturday."

"I picked up some overtime." The gold tooth flashed. "Making a delivery. Your wall is here."

"My…wall?"

"Yup."

"I didn't order a wall, Doug."

"Well, somebody did," the truck driver said cheerfully.

"Where do you want it?"

The screen door opened and Jeremy charged in, Cody and Logan on his heels.

"It's awesome, Kate!"

"When can we climb it?"

"Can I go first?"

Kate walked over to the window and looked outside. Strapped to the back of a flatbed truck were enormous slabs of what appeared to be gray rock.

A climbing wall.

Matt had come up with something guaranteed to rival Dev McGuire's survival skills presentation.

She allowed the boys to herd her outside, prodded along by their excited chatter. Several of the adult mentors had hopped on the back of the truck and started to remove the pieces. Matt broke away from the group and jogged over when he saw them.

"Great idea," Kate said.

Matt's eyebrows shot up. "I was about to say the same thing to you."

"I didn't order this. I could never..." Afford to rent a climbing wall for the afternoon.

But Kate knew someone who could.

Alex finished a spot-check on the last cabin and headed back to the lodge. As he emerged from the trees, he saw the boys stampeding down to the lake.

Matt and some of the other adult volunteers took up the rear, waving their arms in the air to keep the stragglers moving.

Cody Lang slowed down as he passed Alex and pointed to the climbing wall. He gave him a thumbs-up sign.

Alex had told Doug that he preferred to be

an anonymous benefactor; but, in hindsight, realized he probably should have said: "Don't tell anyone I set this up."

The wall had been a hit. For the majority of the afternoon, both the boys and their mentors had climbed it. The shouts of encouragement and cheers had been so boisterous that several fishermen had putted over to see what the ruckus was about.

"Okay, everyone listen up!" Matt said as the boys collapsed on the grass at the edge of the water. "We're going to have a contest."

Curious, Alex paused at the perimeter of the group to listen.

"Here are the rules." Matt's gaze swept over the group. "Each of you will have twenty minutes to build a sand castle with your mentor. One bucket per team. You can't build your castle more than three feet from the water or you'll be disqualified."

Alex frowned. Talk about setting the kids up for failure. They'd be fighting a losing battle with the waves that lapped at the shoreline.

Not that it was his problem. The celebrity who'd complained about the dripping faucet in the presidential suite at Porter Grand was his problem.

Logan suddenly detached from the group and began to slink away, a dejected look on his face.

"Logan?" Alex caught up with the boy in two strides. "Aren't you going to build a castle?"

"You have to have a partner."

"What about Pastor Wilde?" Alex couldn't imagine the guy turning Logan away just because he hadn't been officially teamed up with one of the adults in the mentoring ministry.

"Cody asked him already." The toe of Logan's tennis shoe sliced through the grass. "I don't care. It's his picnic."

Alex read between the lines. Cody belonged and he didn't.

It looked as though the celebrity would have to wait.

"It's been a long time, but I think I can build a sand castle," he said slowly.

"Really?" The boy's face lit up.

"Sure. Come on." Time to mentally blow the dust off his bachelor's degree.

"Okay!" Logan trotted down to the edge of the water, where Matt and Harold Davis were in the process of cordoning off a section of the beach with a bright orange towrope.

Alex got Matt's attention. "Mind if we crash your contest?"

"The more the merrier."

"You do realize the waves are going to reach your three-foot mark," Alex said in a low voice.

"Yup," Matt said cheerfully.

And here he'd thought the guy was normal. For a preacher.

"At least we're straight on that," Alex muttered.

Logan was issued a bucket and a flimsy plastic shovel. He would have started to fill it with sand if Alex hadn't stopped him.

"The waves are going to wash it away unless we put something solid underneath it."

"Like what?"

"Wood. Sticks. Anything like that."

"I'll find some." Logan dashed off.

While the other teams got right down to the business of piling bucketfuls of sand in one place, Alex showed Logan how to create a raised platform out of the mismatched driftwood.

"We're going to run out of time," Logan fretted.

"We'll be fine."

Less than ten minutes later, Harold Davis blew his whistle.

"Time's up and it's time to eat!"

Sand sprayed the air as the boys made a mad dash to the picnic tables, the contest forgotten for the moment.

"Ours isn't the biggest," Logan muttered as he and Alex walked past the castles dotting the shoreline. "We're not going to win."

Alex winked at him.

"Trust me."

Kate tracked her cell phone to the table on the deck and scooped it up right before it went to voice mail.

"Hello?"

"Hey, Kate."

Grace.

Ordinarily, Kate would have been thrilled to hear from her friend. But because that friend was also Tori and Logan's caseworker, a trickle of unease scrambled up her spine.

"Do you have a minute?"

Kate anchored the phone against her shoulder and bent down to pick up a piece of watermelon rind before it attracted every ant in the county. "Sure. Tori went down for a nap a few minutes ago."

"She hasn't been sleeping well at night?"

Kate bit her lip. Leave it to a professional to read between the lines. "Not really, but last night was better."

Because she had taken Alex's advice and plugged in a nightlight.

"I'm not surprised." Grace sighed. "I visited their home yesterday. The fire only caused minor damage in the living room so all it needs is to air out and get a good cleaning. The fire chief gave the okay for them to move back in when it's time."

"Do you know when that will be?" Kate knew this moment would come but she hadn't realized how much she'd been dreading it.

"I talked to Jenna Gardner this morning. Apparently she hasn't heard from her sister since Logan was born. She seemed pretty upset when I told her what happened."

Upset enough to come to her niece and nephew's aid?

"Does she *want* them?"

Grace hesitated. "She wants to do what's right."

Was that the same thing? Kate wasn't sure.

Grace read her mind. "You know I won't place Tori and Logan with their aunt if I don't feel it's the best situation."

"I know." Kate pushed the words past the lump in her throat.

"I'll call you as soon as I have more information," Grace promised. "Keep praying and don't worry. God has those two kids in the palm of His hand and He won't drop them."

"I know." Kate blinked back a fresh coat of tears as she hung up the phone.

She knew the children would be leaving but she hadn't realized how difficult it would be.

Grace is right, God, but Tori and Logan have been through so much. They need stability. They need someone who will listen to them and read them stories and love them— Kate stopped and smiled in the middle of the prayer. *I'm sorry, Lord. I'm not telling You anything that You don't already know.*

Her smile grew wider as her gaze fell on Alex, who sat cross-legged on a picnic blanket next to Logan, listening intently to something the boy was saying.

God had already provided the very things Kate had just asked for.

In a very unexpected way.

Alex Porter wasn't the only one with a "grand plan." If only he would begin to see that God's was the only one worth seeking.

Chapter Eighteen

Matt blew the whistle around his neck to signal the end of the lunch break.

"Ready to find out who won our castle building contest?"

The boys yelled and pumped the air with their fists. An enthusiastic response that quickly faded to disappointment when they ran down to the lake.

The waves had eroded their best efforts.

"Half of it washed away," Alex heard one of the boys complain.

"Ours didn't," Logan whispered, his eyes round with astonishment.

Alex smiled and put a finger to his lips as

Matt motioned for all the boys to sit down in a circle around him.

"I'd like to read something to you." The pastor pulled a small leather book from the back pocket of his jeans and thumbed through it.

"Jesus spoke these words a long time ago, but the thing about God's word is that it never goes out of style, kind of like the shoes Zach likes to wear."

Zach Davis grinned and lifted one of his size thirteen feet so the group could admire his Hi-Top Chuck Taylor All Stars.

Matt waited until the giggling died down before his gaze dropped to the worn Bible cradled in his palm.

"Therefore everyone who hears these words of mine and puts them into practice is like a wise man who built his house on the rock. The rain came down, the streams rose, and the winds blew and beat against that house, yet it did not fall, because it had its foundation on the rock."

Matt paced down the beach and stopped up short beside the only sand castle that had remained intact.

"Who built this one?"

Alex nodded at Logan and the boy tentatively lifted his hand.

"Me and Alex."

"It didn't wash away like the rest of them." Matt looked a little astounded.

"We put sticks down before we built it," Logan said, his cheeks turning red from being the center of attention.

Matt's lips twitched. "Well, let's call this Exhibit A. I wasn't expecting this, but we're going to go with it."

"He's an architect," Logan said with a hint of pride that stained *Alex's* cheeks red.

"I'll read the rest of the passage now and I think it's safe to say that we can label the other castles Exhibit B."

Still smiling, Matt glanced down at the passage once again. "But everyone who hears these words of mine and does not put them into practice is like a foolish man who built his house on the sand. The rain came down, the streams rose, and the winds blew and beat against that house, and it fell with a great crash."

He closed the Bible.

"Jesus told this story to a crowd of people— if I had to guess, I'd say some of them were boys, like you. He wanted them to know that what a man builds his life on matters. It's the foundation that determines whether a house will stand during the hard times, not what it's made out of.

"When you built your castle, you mixed together the right combination of water and sand. Maybe you even added a few sticks and rocks to make it look good. But what made them all collapse? The fact that you built them on sand."

"You told us to!" one of the older boys shouted.

"Exactly." Matt looked pleased rather than annoyed by the comment. "A lot of people are going to tell you that in order to be successful in life you have to build your life on something other than Jesus. But He's our rock. Our foundation. A relationship with Him is the only thing that will keep us strong. Keep us from falling apart when things get tough. It's the only thing that lasts."

Matt let his gaze touch each boy in the

circle as he slipped the New Testament into his pocket.

"Let's close our time together with a word of prayer."

"He's sneaky," one of the boys next to Alex whispered.

Alex had been thinking the same thing.

Matt bowed his head and said a short prayer, thanking God for His faithfulness, fellowship and the food He had provided. The boys' rousing amen served as the benediction.

"And speaking of food, Kate has ice-cream sundaes for everyone," Harold Davis announced with a wide smile.

Cody Lang, who'd been sitting near them, leaped to his feet. "Come on, Logan."

Logan looked at Alex, a question in his eyes.

"Go ahead. I'll be right there."

Matt grabbed an end of the tow rope and began to wind it up. "Something on your mind, Alex?"

"You're good, I'll give you that much."

"Thanks. I guess that means I'll see you in church tomorrow morning."

Alex, who'd bent down to pick up an empty soda bottle, shot the pastor a wry glance.

Really good.

Matt gestured toward the castle Alex and Logan had built. "I appreciate the prop, by the way. I figured all of them would have collapsed by the time we finished dinner but I didn't know I had an architect in the group."

"I'm not an architect."

"Maybe not," Matt said easily. "But you knew the castle needed a foundation."

The irony wasn't lost on Alex. When it came to building a sand castle, he'd known exactly what to do. He wasn't so sure he could say the same thing about his life. Not anymore.

The night before, he had asked a question.

Are You trying to tell me something, Lord?

Sidestepping a wave that dissolved half of the castle next to his foot, Alex figured he'd just received the answer.

Now he had to decide what he was going to do about it.

Kate plunged her hands into the soapy dishwater and closed her eyes.

The bubbles…the soothing hot water… both reminded her how long it had been since she'd taken a long, therapeutic soak in the tub. Showers didn't count. In, shampoo, condition and out. The drive-thru of cleanliness.

The housekeeping staff had returned at promptly six o'clock and swept away the remains of the picnic and left her with nothing but a few stray coffee cups to wash.

Thanks to Alex, the man who had predicted she would be too tired to change her mind by the end of the day.

Kate didn't want to thank Alex. She didn't want to see him, either. Not while her emotions simmered just below the surface of her skin, ready to bubble up at a moment's notice.

Every time she looked at Tori and Logan, Kate wanted to wrap her arms around them and hold on tight. Promise them that everything would be okay.

She wanted to believe that for herself, too. But something told her that Tori and Logan weren't the only ones who would create a void in her life when they were gone.

A week ago, Kate would have thought she'd

be counting the hours until Alex returned to Chicago, but now all she wanted to do was make them last a little longer.

She needed a cup of tea. And chocolate.

"I should have known you'd be in here."

Alex's rough velvet voice tugged at the edges of her already frayed emotions.

Hot tears poked the backs of Kate's eyes, proof that she needed to curl up with her Bible and soak in God's promises even more than she needed a long soak in the tub.

"Tori and Logan are watching a movie. They're both pretty tuckered out." Making small talk was safer than the alternative. Falling apart in front of Alex.

"I just checked on them." Alex wandered into the kitchen, looking like the cover model for an issue of *Outdoor Millionaire Monthly.* Hair ruffled by the wind. A faint grain of stubble on his angular jaw.

It wasn't fair that he smelled terrific, too. Like fresh cedar boughs and sunshine.

After an hour spent flipping burgers and brats on the grill, Kate was pretty sure she smelled like Smoky the Bear's prom date.

Alex picked a cup out of the drainer and put it away. "Tori fell asleep on the sofa. Do you want me to carry her upstairs?"

The Gardner siblings weren't Alex's responsibility and yet he'd spent the entire afternoon with Logan. And now he was offering to help her with Tori.

All Kate could do was nod. "Thank you."

She dried her hands on a towel and followed him into the gathering room, where an antique armoire harbored a flat-screen television.

"I'm going to carry your sister upstairs so Kate can put her to bed, if that's okay with you, Logan," Alex said in a low voice.

This was the man that Kate had labeled "insensitive."

When Logan nodded, Alex gathered Tori into his arms, blanket and all, and made the trek to the third floor as easily as if he were carrying a feather.

Logan trailed behind them, one yawn tumbling after the other like dominoes.

"Sounds like you're ready for bed, too," Kate whispered.

"I'm gonna read for a while."

Kate tried not to chuckle when the boy picked up Abby's worn copy of *How to Survive and Thrive in the Woods* and disappeared into his room.

Alex laid Tori down on the bed. "I'll let you take it from here."

The little girl stirred and opened her eyes. "Mommy?"

Kate's heart broke when she saw Tori's gaze dart around the room, desperately searching for something familiar.

"Would you like me to sit with you awhile?" When Tori nodded, Kate sat down on the bed. Tori immediately snuggled up next to her and Kate wrapped an arm around her thin shoulders.

An hour later, she stumbled toward the kitchen and ran into Alex instead.

Kate had planned to take a walk to clear her head and here he was, standing in her way, threatening to muddle it again. Ordinarily, she faced a tough situation head-on; but tonight it felt as if her heart was beating on the outside of her chest, bruised and exposed.

She didn't want to think about losing Tori and Logan.

Or Alex.

"Come with me."

Kate tried to muster some indignation at his autocratic tone but was too tired. She thought they were going to his office, but Alex turned in the direction of the kitchen.

Had Mulligan and Lady been playing tug-of-war with the scatter rug?

Was Mrs. Avocado acting up again?

"Sit."

Kate scowled at him. "You really have to stop watching reruns of *The Dog Whisperer.*"

"*Please* sit down. Is that better?"

"Alex." Kate balked in the doorway. She couldn't pretend anymore. "I'm really tired."

"I know." His hands lightly cupped her shoulders and he steered her toward the table.

The gentle touch made Kate's knees buckle and she slid bonelessly into the closest chair.

"Do you want to talk about it?"

"No." She closed her eyes.

"Kate? Look at me. Please," he added.

"Fine. But only because you said the magic word," she muttered.

When she opened her eyes, there was a bowl sitting in front of her.

She blinked. "Is that chocolate chip cookie dough?"

"It's truth serum, only…chunkier." Alex handed her a spoon. "I discovered it when Abby was a teenager. She would tell me everything when I made up a batch of the stuff. Now take a bite."

Kate did. And a tear leaked out of the corner of her eye. His kindness was going to snip the last thread of her self-control.

"Now, tell me what's bothering you?"

"Grace called this afternoon while you were outside with Logan."

Was it her imagination, or did she see a spark of concern in Alex's eyes?

"What did she say?"

"Their aunt, Jenna Gardner, wants the weekend to decide what to do. She hasn't seen the children since Logan was born. What if she wants to take them back to Minnesota with her? They don't even *know* her, Alex. They need stability and love, not to be uprooted again."

"You want to keep them."

Leave it to Alex to cut to the heart of the matter.

"Yes. But I can't. I'm not certified for long-term foster care." Kate sighed. "Like you said, my apartment is too small. There's no yard."

"Get something bigger."

"Spoken like a man who has a house on every continent."

"Not *every* continent."

Kate caught her bottom lip between her teeth. "I've always wanted a house, but I can't afford one. Every spare penny goes in a savings account for the café."

"You want to renovate it?"

Tell him, Kate.

"I want to buy it back."

Alex frowned as the words sunk in.

"I thought your father left the café to you when he moved to Arizona."

"That's what everyone thinks. But Dad wouldn't have been able to start over there unless he sold the café *here,* so he made a deal with a local investor. Jeff agreed to let me manage the café as if it were mine. Kind of a silent partnership."

"Jeff?" Alex's gut tightened.

Kate nodded. "Jeff Gaines. He wanted to remain anonymous because he wasn't sure how the community would respond to an outsider—a lot of people weren't too happy with him because he was scoping out land for his condos at the time. He told Dad that he wanted to support local businesses so it was a good deal for all of us."

Alex knew better. No matter how a positive spin the guy had put on it, Gaines had definitely come out ahead. Kate put everything she had into the business, drawing a modest salary, while Jeff sat back and took in the profit.

"The contract states that if Jeff ever decides to sell, I will be given the opportunity to buy the Grapevine first," Kate continued. "My dream has always been to buy him out when I had the money, so that's where the money goes."

That explained the apartment and the lack of updates in the diner.

The conversation had taken an entirely different path than Alex had anticipated. He'd seen Kate's expression when Tori had cried out for her mother. She wanted to do everything possible to protect the children in her care.

And he wanted to see her smile again.

"Let's break this down, shall we?" Alex said slowly. "You don't know what their aunt is like, so try not to assume the worst because she has to think about the commitment she's making. Some people are planners and it's not always a bad thing."

Judging from the expression on her face, Kate understood his meaning.

"And from the mini sermons my sister likes to preach, you're supposed to trust God that He has a plan, too."

Kate's mouth dropped open.

"You're telling me to trust God?"

"I'm *reminding* you."

"You don't play fair."

"That's only for you superheroes." Alex shrugged. "No one ever said that we evil geniuses had to."

There it was. The smile he'd been waiting for.

"Evil genius, huh?" Kate tipped her head. "Well, let's break this down, *shall* we?"

Alex had a feeling she was about to turn the tables on him.

"You rented a climbing wall today so the boys wouldn't be disappointed—"

"I was worried they'd be climbing the trees if they didn't have something to occupy their time."

Kate ignored that. "And you entered the sand castle contest with Logan—"

"Because I like to win." Alex's lip curled at the corner. "And we did."

"I hate to break this to you, Alex, but all that *and* mixing up a batch of cookie dough while you listened to my problems? Very heroic."

"Heroic?"

"Heroic," Kate repeated firmly. "If you keep this up, you're going to need a cape, too." She saw his expression and the smile bloomed brighter. "Don't look so disappointed. You know what they say about nice guys."

"They finish last?"

"Don't be so cynical. It's not becoming in a superhero." Kate took another spoonful and then stared at it, her brow puckering. "Wait a second. What's in this stuff? I told you about the café and no one, not even my closest friends, know that I'm the manager, not the owner."

"Truth serum, only—"

"Chunkier. Got it."

"You're finishing my sentences again. You must be feeling better."

"I am." Kate rose to her feet and went up on her tiptoes. Curved her hands around his biceps to steady herself as she looked him straight in the eye. "Thank you."

Alex could walk into those clover-green eyes and not care if he ever found his way out again.

Last night, only sheer willpower and a healthy dose of self-preservation had prevented Alex from taking her into his arms.

"I just remembered something else about good guys."

"What's that?" Kate looked suspicious now.

She would have stepped back but Alex slipped his arms around her waist.

Kate's lips parted in surprise, which worked to Alex's advantage.

"They get the girl."

He bent his head and kissed her.

Chapter Nineteen

Kate was the one who broke away first—several moments after she'd melted against him and returned the kiss.

She pressed the tips of her fingers against her lips.

"What. Was. That?"

"If you have to ask, I must not have done it right." Laughter gleamed in his eyes and for a split second, Kate thought Alex was going to take her into his arms for an instant replay.

She backpedaled to put some distance between them.

He raked a hand through his hair. "Would you like me to say I'm sorry?"

Kate bit her lip. "Are you?"

"No."

"Oh." *Oh.*

"You?"

Kate found herself wishing she wasn't such a stickler for honesty. "No."

They stared at each other uncertainly, each waiting for the other one to explain what had just happened. And why.

"I think I'm better at arguing." Kate sighed.

Alex flashed a smile that could only be described as rakish. "You're good at both."

"I didn't mean…I'm not…" Could the floor just open up and swallow her whole now?

Did Alex think she was the kind of girl who treated kissing with the same lighthearted attitude as shopping for shoes?

"I'm sure this is something you're…used to," Kate stammered. "But I don't—"

"Neither do I." Alex interrupted. And for some odd reason, Kate believed him.

He closed the distance between them in one stride. "Kate, I've never felt like this before…" He cringed. "The fact that I'm quoting a line from one of those cheesy date movies is your proof."

"I love those movies."

Alex reached out his hand and hooked a curl behind her ear. "I didn't plan this."

Kate believed that, too. Because Kate wasn't the kind of woman who turned the heads of men like Alex Porter. Her clothes didn't have designer labels and she entered pies in the county fair.

"I know." Kate swallowed hard. "It was sweet of you to comfort me."

Alex's eyes widened. "You think that was a *pity* kiss?"

"Well. I was upset."

"Now I *know* I didn't do it right," Alex muttered.

Before Kate could protest—not that she would have—he pulled her into his arms and kissed her again. Quite thoroughly.

When they finally parted, Kate's feet had melted into the floor.

"The cookie dough was to comfort you." Alex's voice sounded a little unsteady. "The kiss was because you're beautiful—"

Beautiful?

"—and because I care about you." Before Kate could react, Alex framed her face in his hands and pressed a kiss against her forehead. "To prove it, I'm going to be one of the good guys you just claimed I was and say good night now."

A low rumble of thunder woke Alex up the following morning.

Not that he'd slept much.

After Kate went upstairs, he'd taken the dogs outside and walked down to the lake. Moonlight dappled the shoreline where the waves had washed the sand castles away.

Like his best-laid plans.

Alex turned his head toward the rain-spattered window.

In one short week, it seemed as if everything was conspiring against him.

Or maybe *for* him.

For the first time, Alex was actually willing to entertain the idea.

He hadn't planned on Kate, though. She was like a song he wanted to play over and over again until he learned every note.

Alex hadn't planned to kiss her, either; but once he had, he couldn't let her think that he had done so because he felt sorry for her.

He had realized something was bothering

Kate during the picnic. Her usual buoyancy had deflated like a helium balloon with a hole in it. While she'd put the Tori to bed, he had mixed up a batch of the eggless cookie dough that Abby had loved.

Women and chocolate.

No one could accuse him of not paying attention.

He had hoped Kate would confide in him but he hadn't expected her to take it a step further.

Frowning, Alex rolled out of bed and snagged a pair of jeans from the top drawer of the dresser.

He had assumed that Kate's decision to stay in Mirror Lake and run the café was born from a desire to carry on the family business. But technically, it no longer fell under that category.

So why had she stayed? Why was she managing the Grapevine for a silent partner when she could be doing so much more?

He'd just finished getting dressed when he heard a soft tap on the door.

"Knock, knock."

Alex smiled. "Who's there?"

"Lettuce," came the whispered reply.

"Lettuce who?"

"Lettuce eat cake."

Alex opened the door and scooped Tori up in his arms. "For breakfast?"

"No, we ate scrambled eggs and toast." She giggled as he tossed her over one shoulder and toted her down the stairs. "We're goin' to church now."

Church.

I'm not ready for that yet, God, Alex thought.

But then, he wasn't ready for a lot of things. He wasn't ready to admit he'd been wrong about some of the decisions he'd made. He wasn't ready to let go of the past because he wasn't sure what he would hold on to.

And he wasn't ready to fall in love even though he had a strong suspicion it had already happened...

"Tori? Logan? It looks like we're going to be late." Kate was peeling off a yellow slicker as she came down the hall. Raindrops winked in her hair.

She stopped short when she saw him.

"Good morning."

Kate had to look at him now. And she blushed the color of a new penny.

Alex *knew* she would blush.

"What's the matter?"

"Thor wants to sleep in this morning."

"He won't start," Alex guessed.

"Exactly." Kate pulled out her cell. "I'm going to call Emma. If she and Jake haven't left already, they can stop and pick us up on their way into town."

Thunder rumbled again and Tori clung to him. "I don't like that noise," she whimpered.

Alex tapped her button nose. "The storm is on the outside and you're on the inside," he said. "There's nothing to be afraid of."

Kate closed her phone and sighed. "There's no answer. They must have left early."

"You can take Abby's convertible," Alex offered. "It's parked in the garage."

"Really? You don't think she'd mind?"

"I know she wouldn't. The keys are in the desk drawer."

Kate sprang into action. "I'll be right back. Tori, can you find your brother and tell him we're leaving, please?"

"Okay." But instead of scurrying away to

find Logan, the little girl lingered when Alex set her down on the floor. "I'm going to color a picture in Sunday school. We sing songs and get to hear a story, too."

"You like stories."

"Uh-huh." Tori sounded a little uncertain, leading Alex to believe that she wasn't too sure about church, either.

He could relate.

"You met Pastor Matt yesterday, remember? He's the one who tells the stories." And Alex had to admit the guy was pretty good at it.

"Okay." Tori didn't look totally convinced, but she scampered off to get Logan, and Alex intercepted Kate at the front door.

"I'll get the car and bring it around."

"You don't have to." Her fingers curled around the keys.

"That's not what the hero handbook says. Do you want me to earn my badge or not?"

"Fine. You win."

"Music to my ears."

So was Kate's laughter when she dropped the car keys into his outstretched palm.

A shard of lightning split the sky as Alex

pulled up in front of the door. He heard Tori shriek and saw her scuttle backward.

"I don't want to go out there," she was saying as Alex jogged to the doorway.

Kate knelt down beside her. "Do you want to hold the umbrella?"

"No," Tori wailed.

The trees bowed under a gust of wind and Alex scooped the little girl up, shielding her under his coat.

"You can sit in the backseat with her," he told Kate. "I'll drop you off at the church."

Before she could protest, he returned to the car and buckled Tori into her booster. Logan joined him in the front seat, grinning even as raindrops dripped off the end of his nose. "This car is so awesome."

"So is Thor," Kate murmured. "When he wants to be."

Alex grinned.

People were still dodging raindrops when he pulled up to the front doors of the little white church a few minutes later.

Alex glanced over his shoulder at Kate. "I'll be back after the service."

"Aren't you coming with us?" Logan looked concerned.

"No." Alex hadn't stepped foot in a church since his parents' funeral. "I'll pick you up after the service, though."

"Kate says that it's important to come to church because God likes to see His family get together," Logan said seriously.

Alex had never heard it put like that before but it sounded like something Kate would say.

"She's right." Alex winced. Because those words weren't going to come back to haunt him later!

"Don't you like stories?" Tori cast a nervous glance at the church, as if she were wondering why Alex didn't want to go inside and maybe she should stay in the car, too?

"I do like stories," he heard himself say.

"And you like Pastor Matt." Unblinking, periwinkle eyes met his.

"Yes."

Tori lifted her arms toward him, as if that settled the matter.

He looked at Kate, who was trying hard to

look sympathetic to his plight. "It looks like I'm going to church with you."

She chuckled. "I'm pretty sure that was the plan all along."

"Yours?" Had Kate fibbed about her car not starting, hoping that he would take them to church?

Kate simply smiled at him. "God's."

Kate resisted the urge to pinch herself as she sat down. In the pew. Next to Alex.

She could feel the curious looks from the people around them as Tori climbed onto her lap and Logan exchanged a whispered conversation with Jeremy Sutton.

Friends paused to say hello and smiled at Alex, greeting him by name as if they had seen him in church a dozen times.

Kate could practically feel the tension radiating from Alex. How long had it been since he'd attended a worship service? Abby had said she remembered going to church on Christmas Eve with her parents, but that Alex had chosen to stay home.

God, it isn't an accident or a coincidence that Alex is here this morning. Help him see

*that You are real and that You love him. Help
him put the past to rest and trust You with his
future.*

Alex smiled at something that Tori said,
forcing Kate to add a hasty amendment to
her prayer.

*I need to trust You with my future, too,
Lord.*

Even if it didn't include Alex.

Kate closed the hymnal and as the notes
of the last song ended, silently thanked God
that all four of them had made it through the
service.

Well, almost all of them. Tori had fallen
asleep in her arms during the sermon but
Logan hadn't fidgeted and Alex hadn't
walked out during the message.

As they rose to their feet for the benediction, Kate glanced at Alex. It was difficult
to read his expression. Matt's sermons were
always easy for the mind to grasp but had a
way of cutting straight to the soul.

He'd read Jesus' parable about the two men
who'd built houses—one on sand and the
other on a rock. As an illustration, Matt had

told the congregation about the castle building contest at the inn the day before.

Logan had tugged on Alex's sleeve when
he mentioned a certain team who'd actually
built their castle on a foundation.

Once again, God's sense of humor made
Kate smile. Alex, a man who wasn't sure
about God, had provided the example of a
life of faith.

Mr. Lundy paused beside their pew.

"I'll see you after church, Kate." He patted
the case that held his chess set before turning to Alex. "I'm looking forward to another
game."

Kate had completely forgotten about her
weekly dinner.

Between the picnic, taking care of Tori and
Logan and running back and forth between
the café and the inn, it had totally slipped her
mind.

"So am I." Kate smiled. "I'll see you at the
apartment."

"Why didn't you tell Mr. Lundy that you
canceled it today?" Alex murmured when
Arthur shuffled away.

"Ah… Because I didn't?"

"You're cooking dinner at your apartment?"

"We need to eat anyway. I'll come up with something." At the moment, Kate had no idea what. "Just drop me and the kids off at my apartment on your way back to the inn."

"It's raining."

"And thunnering," Tori chimed in.

Thank goodness for five-year-old eavesdroppers, Kate thought. They forced one to mind their manners.

"You don't have the roof as overflow," Alex said mildly, although Kate saw a flash of lightning in his eyes.

"It'll be cozy."

"Cozy." The tone carried a similar inflection Kate heard when people said "mosquitoes" or "poison ivy."

Fortunately, Zoey came to her rescue.

"Hey, Kate. The Kid's Club is having a scavenger hunt tomorrow morning. I thought maybe Tori and Logan would like to come while you're at the café."

"That sounds great."

"I'll add their names to the list." Zoey smiled. "See you in a little while."

Kate ignored Alex's growl.

"Kate?" Morgan trotted up to her. "Can you come down to the youth wing for a sec? I need your help with something."

"Sure." In for a penny, in for a pound, as her mom used to say.

Twenty minutes later, she and Alex loaded the children into the car and headed back to the apartment.

"Are you sure you don't want to stop at a deli and pick up something to eat?" Alex asked.

"Number one, Mirror Lake doesn't have a deli. And number two, it wouldn't be as good as what I can make."

"What are you making, by the way?"

"It's a secret recipe."

Alex slanted a look at her as he pulled into the alley. "That means you don't know, either."

Kate resisted the urge to stick out her tongue. Because it was important to provide a good role model for children.

While Alex helped Tori out of the backseat, Kate bounded up the stairs and opened the door.

"There you are! Hope you don't mind that we let ourselves in!"

Kate's mouth dropped open as she took in the scene.

A crowd of people were moving around her apartment like worker ants. Setting out dishes. Lining up steaming casserole dishes along the counter. The centerpiece on the table was a triple-layer cake with waves of butter cream frosting.

Several of the teens from her youth group were sprawled on the floor, playing with the cats. Mr. Lundy was setting up the chess pieces.

"What's going on?" Kate moved forward when she felt Alex's gentle nudge against the small of her back.

"We know you've been busy this week, so we decided to make dinner," Esther Redstone sang out.

"But instead of going to one country, we're going all the way around the world," Delia said. "Everyone brought a dish to pass."

"I can't believe you went to all this trouble."

"Trouble?" Delia snorted. "We're being selfish, sweetie. Sunday afternoons would get downright lonely if it weren't for you opening up your home."

"You take care of us, we take care of you." Rose Williams swept past with a basket of sourdough rolls. "That's the way it works."

Kate sneaked a glance at Alex.

He had stalked over to the table to inspect the variety of dishes that could be created with a pound of hamburger and a can of cream of mushroom soup.

"You look a little shocked, Mr. Porter." Delia's pink cane lifted and administered an affectionate tap on his shoulder. "Is this your first potluck?"

"Um…yes."

"Well today you're going to see what you've been missing," the elderly woman declared.

Looking at Alex's dazed expression, Kate could only hope so.

Chapter Twenty

"You're all set, Ms. Foster. If you need anything, please let me know." Alex held out the key to cabin four.

"There's no need to be so formal, Alex," Blaire Foster purred. "And I'm sure everything will be wonderful. It isn't exactly Porter Lakeside, but it has its own charm, I suppose."

She took the key and the tips of her perfectly manicured, blood-red nails reminded Alex of talons. "Who knows? Maybe I'll extend my stay for a few days."

There was no mistaking the meaning. Or the subtle invitation in the curve of her lips.

If Alex had known who was waiting for

him at the front desk to check in, he would have been tempted to hide in the kitchen. Blaire Foster had pursued him for several months, but because she had reverted to her maiden name following a recent divorce, Alex hadn't made the connection until she had sashayed up to the reservation desk like a runway model.

Blaire was stunning, there was no doubt about it. At one time, Alex might have considered asking her out to dinner.

Instead, he smiled politely.

"Another guest already reserved your cabin for tomorrow night." And the three hundred and sixty-four after that.

Blaire pouted. "You can't make an exception for a close friend?"

Maybe he could, if a close friend was the one asking.

"No, I'm sorry."

Blaire parked a hand on her hip, a calculated pose designed to accentuate her willowy figure. "If you get lonely this afternoon, my cabin has a great view of the lake."

Alex saw a flash of metal as a '57 Thunderbird coasted up the driveway.

"Thank you, but I've got a great view from here." Alex watched a petite redhead bounce out of the front seat and his mood improved.

Blaire narrowed her eyes.

"You seem different, Alex."

Alex smiled.

"Thank you."

Blaire looked a little bewildered as she walked toward the door.

Alex heard Kate and Blaire exchange a greeting as they passed each other on the walkway outside. There were only three guests scheduled to arrive, so Kate had opted to spend the morning at the café, catching up on some paperwork and reordering supplies.

He'd missed her.

The door opened and she plunged into the lobby. Alex took in her expression and went cold. Her eyes were dark with emotion, her freckles stood out in sharp relief against the pallor of her skin.

Concern propelled Alex around the reservation desk. "What's wrong? Where are Tori and Logan?"

"They're still with Zoey at the church."

"Did you talk to the social worker again?"

Alex went to touch her arm but she shied away from him.

"Can we talk in your office?" she asked in a tight voice.

"Of course." Alex ushered her down the hall and closed the door. "What happened, Kate?"

Kate couldn't believe he had the audacity to ask.

"This morning, I got a call from Jeff Gaines while I was at work. He's given me twenty-four hours to come up with the money to buy the café or it's going to be sold to someone else."

"Twenty-four hours," he repeated. "Isn't that going to be difficult?"

"Difficult?" Kate's voice cracked on the word. "Try impossible. A down payment I might have been able to manage, but he wants the entire amount."

"Why would he do that?"

"You tell me." The tears Kate had been battling surfaced. How could Alex stand there and look so calm? As if he hadn't been responsible for destroying everything she'd worked for.

His mouth fell open. "You don't think I had something to do with this?"

"Did you talk to Jeff?"

His expression became guarded. "Kate—"

"Did you talk to Jeff? It's a yes or no question."

"Yes, but we didn't…" Alex hesitated and Kate could almost see the wheels turning in his head. "It's not what you're thinking."

"You didn't tell Jeff that I was wasting my talent? That I could do so much more with my life if I wasn't 'tied down' by the café?"

Kate saw the truth in his eyes and felt the bottom drop out of her world. Again.

A small part of her had held out hope that Jeff hadn't been parroting Alex's words.

"I might have said those things, but I didn't ask Jeff to sell the café out from under you. I didn't even know he owned it."

"But you found out. Because I *told* you." She'd trusted Alex and he'd used the information against her.

"The conversation I had with Jeff took place last week," Alex said quietly. "I had no idea he was going to do this. You have to believe me."

Kate didn't know what to believe anymore.

Until an hour ago, she wouldn't have believed that Jeff Gaines, the easygoing businessman who sent her flowers on boss's day, would take advantage of a loosely worded contract and destroy her dream.

Kate impatiently dashed away a tear that rolled down her cheek. "Do you know what else Jeff said? He told me that someday I would *thank* him for doing this."

Alex didn't say anything.

"You *agree* with him, don't you?" Kate whispered. The realization turned the knife in her back. "You think that if I didn't have the café, I would move away. Find another job. Don't you understand? Mirror Lake is my *home*. This is where God wants me to be."

And for a fleeting moment, she'd been naive enough to think that Alex wanted to be here, too. With her.

"I'll talk to Jeff."

"It won't do any good. He has another

buyer interested in the café. Someone he's been putting off for a few years."

Until you got involved.

The unspoken words hung in the air between them.

Alex exhaled in frustration. "Maybe I did tell Jeff that you could be doing more, but it's true. You are playing it safe. Your menu is safe. You cook dishes from different countries but you won't travel to those places yourself. I know you—"

"No," Kate interrupted. The word barely broke above a whisper, but Alex froze as if she'd shouted it. "I thought you were beginning to understand…you said you cared…but you don't know me at all."

That's what hurt the most.

Kate walked toward the door and somehow managed to get into her car and drive back to town.

When Jeff had told her that she had twenty-four hours to come up with the money to buy the café, she had imagined that things couldn't get any worse.

She'd been wrong.

As the reality of the situation seeped in,

with it came a bone-chilling numbness. She'd trusted Alex with a confidence she had never shared with her closest friends and he'd used it against her.

Kate drove past the café, unable to face Grady yet. He would take one look at her and know something terrible had occurred.

She was about to lose everything. Her business. Her home.

Alex.

Don't be silly, Kate told herself fiercely. *You can't lose something you never had.*

"You must be looking for Kate."

Alex glanced over his shoulder and saw Matt standing in the doorway of the sanctuary at Church of the Pines.

Was he looking for Kate? Or answers?

"I messed up." There. He'd admitted it.

"Really."

Alex narrowed his eyes. "You don't seem surprised."

Matt smiled. "Not as surprised as you are maybe, but it can't be the first time."

It was the first time Alex had admitted it. No, the second. The first had occurred the summer before, when he'd told Abby that he'd made a mistake in not trusting her judgment.

Matt closed the door and walked down the aisle. Alex half expected the pastor to take his place behind the wooden pulpit but he sat down on the carpeted stair in front of the pew instead.

"Do you want to talk about it?"

"No. Yes." Alex raked a hand through his hair. "I...did something. Something that I'm not sure Kate will forgive me for."

"All right. I'm listening." Matt spoke evenly enough but Alex saw the man's jaw tighten, reminding him that Kate wasn't just a member of the pastor's congregation but a close friend.

That, Alex realized, was the kind of loyalty Kate inspired. That even a man who had dedicated himself to serving God wanted to punch Alex's lights out if he'd hurt her.

"Two nights ago, Kate told me that she doesn't own the Grapevine. Apparently her father needed the money from the sale of the café in order to leave. The person who bought it, Jeff Gaines, agreed to let Kate stay on as manager. He also promised to give her the first option to buy the café if he ever decided to sell. She's been saving for years to make that happen."

"I had no idea," Matt murmured.

Alex felt the impact of the quiet statement. Kate had confided in him—told him something that she'd never shared with even her closest friends. And now she thought he'd used it against her.

"Part of the agreement was that they keep Jeff's involvement a secret. This morning, he called and told Kate that he wanted to sell the café. He gave her twenty-four hours to come up with the entire purchase price."

"Twenty-four hours," Matt echoed. "I'm not sure that's enough time for Kate to apply for a loan."

"It isn't," Alex said flatly.

Matt frowned. "Why would he do that to her?"

"As a favor to me."

Silence swelled, filling the space between them.

"I don't understand," Matt said at length.

"Jeff and I were in the same fraternity, although he was a few years older than me. We kept in touch over the years and I looked him up when I got into town. He happened to call last week and we had a…conversation."

"A conversation in which you asked him to take away the business Kate has poured her heart and soul into?"

Alex flinched but he couldn't blame the pastor for coming to that conclusion. He had built a reputation for basing his decisions on facts rather than feelings.

"I didn't ask him." Alex drove a hand through his hair. "All I said was that Kate's talents were wasted in Mirror Lake. She could be on the corporate fast-track. Attend a cordon bleu school. She could probably run for governor."

"She doesn't want any of those things."

"I realize that." Now. After he had inadvertently destroyed everything Kate had worked for.

But, not only that, Alex was afraid he had destroyed any chance of a future with her. The devastated look on Kate's face when he'd admitted that he agreed with Jeff continued to haunt him.

"You talked to Gaines?"

"I called him on my way here. He won't budge. I planted a seed and he's taking advantage of it." The same thing Alex would have done if their roles were reversed. "He's got in his head that if Kate doesn't have a job, she'll work for me."

"Is that what you want?"

A week ago, Alex would have said yes.

"I want to make this right."

"Maybe you can't."

Alex stared at him. "You're a pastor. Doesn't that mean you have to encourage people?"

"It also means I can't lie."

"I don't know what to do." The words were easier to say than Alex thought they would be.

"God does. Have you asked Him?"

Alex had already bared his conscience— why not his soul?

"I want to trust Him," he said slowly. "But I don't know where to start."

Matt smiled.

"You just did."

Chapter Twenty-One

Kate didn't have time to wonder why Alex's vehicle wasn't parked in its usual spot by the garage—because Grace Eversea was just getting out of hers.

I don't think I can do this right now, Lord!

The caseworker gave Logan and Tori a warm smile as she approached.

"Hey, you two. I thought I'd stop by and see how you were doing."

The children must have sensed it was more than that because Logan stared at his feet and Tori wilted against Kate's side.

"They went to the scavenger hunt at church this morning," she explained.

"I saw that in the bulletin. Was it fun?"

Logan shrugged. "I guess so."

It was all he could talk about on the way back to the inn but Kate saw no point in mentioning that.

"Would you like a glass of lemonade, Grace?"

"Thank you. That sounds wonderful."

They walked up the cobblestone path in silence. Mulligan ambled up to greet them, a tennis ball clamped in his jaws.

"Can I throw the ball for him, Kate?" Logan asked.

"Sure, but don't go down by the water."

"Okay." With a wary glance at Grace, he took his sister firmly by the hand and led her away.

"I'll wait on the deck so I can keep an eye on them," Grace offered.

Kate opened the fridge and saw the plastic container of cookie dough.

Alex's homemade truth serum.

He'd been so sweet that night. Kate had totally let her guard down. Confided in him.

Don't think about it now.

Kate's hands shook as she collected the pitcher and glasses and stepped onto the deck.

Grace brushed a strand of sable hair off her cheek and smiled wryly when Kate set the tray down. "You used to at least *pretend* to be happy to see me."

"I'm sorry." Kate handed her a glass. "I am glad to see you. I just wish it were under different circumstances."

"So do I." Grace lowered her voice as the children ran under the deck, Mulligan in hot pursuit. "But I have to do my job."

"You talked to their aunt?"

"An hour ago."

"She's coming to Mirror Lake, isn't she?"

"Yes," Grace said simply.

"When will she be here?"

"She called me from her cell phone. She's on her way."

"Now?"

"She'll be arriving later this afternoon." Grace sighed. "I know what you're thinking, Kate, but she's Tori and Logan's closest relative."

"A relative who hasn't seen them for years!"

"I had a lengthy conversation with her and Jake ran a thorough background check. She is willing to stay with the children and there's no reason why I shouldn't let her."

Kate could think of several, but none that would convince Grace to change her mind.

"Will you leave them with me until she gets here?"

"When I explained the situation, Jenna asked if she could stay here for a night or two if you have a room available. That way, the children will get to know her and the transition will be easier."

Kate felt weight on her chest ease. "That's a good idea."

"Let me know after you check with Alex." Grace rose to her feet. "I have an appointment in a few minutes, but I'll be back with Jenna. There are some things she and I need to talk about."

Mulligan trotted up the steps and dropped the ball at their feet.

"Where did your playmates go?" Grace bent down to scratch the dog's ear.

Kate walked to the edge of the deck. "Logan? Tori? Miss Eversea has to leave now."

"I just heard them a few minutes ago." Grace slung her purse over her shoulder.

"They like to play hide and seek in the garden." Kate started down the steps and followed one of the paths that wound through the flower beds to the gazebo.

Grace followed, the heels of her cowboy boots clicking against the flagstone. "I don't see them."

Kate tried not to panic. "They have to be close by. Why don't you go down to the boathouse and see if they're with Jeremy and Cody? I'll check inside."

"All right." Grace turned and walked swiftly back the way they had come.

Kate hurried through the lodge, calling their names, but there was no response.

"I can't find them," Grace panted as they met on the deck a few minutes later. "Is it possible they went into one of the cabins?"

"Logan has a thing about strangers," Kate said. "He won't let Tori even *talk* to someone he doesn't know…"

Their eyes met as both women came to the same disturbing conclusion.

"Do you think they overheard us talking about their aunt?"

Kate hoped not.

Because Logan was fiercely protective of his little sister. And relative or not, Jenna Gardner was a stranger.

Alex parked the Viper next to a hunter-green Blazer marked by an official state license plate. He hopped out of the car and strode up to the main lodge.

"Mr. Porter!" Jeremy and Cody rounded the corner and intercepted him at the door.

"Sorry, guys. I have to talk to Kate."

"She's not here," Jeremy panted. "She and Miss Eversea are looking for Tori and Logan."

"What do you mean, 'looking for them'? Where did they go?"

"We're not sure," Cody said. "The last we saw them, they were playing in the garden. Miss Eversea was talking to Kate on the deck for a while and when it was time for her to leave they were gone."

Gone.

"How long ago?"

The boys looked at each other.

"Half an hour," Cody finally guessed.

Alex stared at the lake. He knew the children had strict instructions not to play near the water without an adult, but would they disregard that rule if something had upset them?

"Miss Eversea walked up the trail to see if Logan and Tori went to the chapel. We would have gone with her but Kate asked us to stay here in case they came back."

"What about Kate?"

"She was going to check the fort," Jeremy said. "We took Logan to see it a few days ago, but it's off the trail so I'm not sure if he'd remember the way."

"I'll see if I can find her." Alex forced a smile. "Do what Kate said and stick close to the lodge, okay? We need you here."

"Okay." The boys exchanged worried looks but didn't argue.

Alex jogged toward an opening in the trees on legs that felt as if they were filled with wet sand.

"Kate?" Alex shouted her name as he scaled a fallen log.

He made his way deeper into the woods, retracing the route he'd taken the day he tracked Kate to the tree fort.

Kate was already dealing with the fallout from the devastation he'd created. If anything happened to Logan and his sister...

God, You know where they are. Help us find them.

He paused, trying to get his bearings, and saw a flash of yellow through the trees.

Tori had been wearing Kate's straw hat that morning at breakfast.

He called her name and heard a faint chirp of alarm.

They were running *away* from him.

The skeletal frame of the tree fort was just up ahead and he saw Kate zigzagging through the trees. He caught up to her in no time.

Relief skimmed through her eyes—and then she looked away.

"Did Grace tell you?"

"Jeremy and Cody." Alex took her arm as they waded through the brush. "I just saw them."

"So did I. They're almost to the property line."

"Can you call the owner?"

Kate shook her head. "No one lives there. It's been abandoned for years."

Alex wanted to ask Kate to forgive him but knew it wasn't the right time. They would have time to talk when Tori and Logan were back at the lodge, safe and sound.

"What happened?"

"They overhead Grace and me talking. Their aunt is coming to Mirror Lake this afternoon."

Alex saw Kate's throat convulse and knew she was fighting back tears.

"We'll find them," he promised.

Moments later, the trees thinned out. They waded through a patch of knee-high weeds scattered with auto parts.

"There's the cabin. I hope they didn't go inside." Kate pointed to a dilapidated structure jutting over the water on weathered, bow-legged stilts.

Alex caught a glimpse of Logan as he dived into the front seat of a rusted out vehicle parked under a willow tree.

"They're hiding in that car."

Kate stumbled and Alex automatically

reached out to steady her. She spun away from him.

No less than he deserved...

But Kate wasn't looking at him. Her gaze remained fixed on the car, every speck of color draining from her face.

"Kate? What is it?"

Her lips formed a single word.

Bees.

She lurched forward, arms and legs churning like windmills as she cut through the knee-length grass.

Alex followed, panic expanding inside his chest and crowding the breath from his lungs when he saw a dark cloud of insects exit through a hole in the broken windshield like a spray of buckshot.

"Don't..." Alex snagged Kate's hand but she shook him off.

"The lake," she gasped. "We've got to get them to the lake."

"*No!* You stay here. I've got them." Alex prayed Kate would listen as he surged ahead of her. The children's muffled screams pierced the air as he raced across the yard and wrenched the car door open.

Logan was curled up on the shredded upholstery, red welts rising on both arms as he swatted the bees away from his sister.

"Come on!" Alex felt the first sting, a hot needle stabbing into his hand, and hauled Logan out of the car where Kate was waiting to transport him to the lake.

The angry hum, rising in intensity, drowned out Tori's sobs. Alex reached in, ignoring the multiple stab wounds the bees were inflicting, and scooped her up. Her arms locked around his neck as he pulled her to safety.

The bees followed.

Tori buried her face against his chest as Alex carried her toward the water. Halfway there, the ground began to shift beneath him.

Alex stumbled and felt Tori slide from his grip. She tried to cling to him, but he set her down and gave her a nudge toward the lake.

"Run to Kate," he muttered, the words sticking in his throat.

Tori broke away from him, shrieking.

Alex's vision blurred and he pitched forward into the sun-scorched grass, his cheek colliding with the ground.

What was happening to him?

He tried to push himself up but it took too much effort.

"Alex."

Dragging in a breath, he saw Kate's face shimmering above him. Felt her hands touching him. Watched her beautiful green eyes darken with alarm—and then fear.

There was so much Alex wanted to say but panic jumbled his thoughts, distilling them down to one thing.

"Forgive—" His throat closed around the word and Alex wasn't sure if it had even made it past his lips.

"I'm calling for help," he heard Kate say. At least he thought it was Kate. What he heard was a thin, shaky echo of the familiar lilting voice.

A thick gray curtain began to slide between them.

He couldn't see Kate anymore. Couldn't feel her.

Couldn't breathe.

Kate could hear the bees.

Hundreds—no, *thousands*—of them. Descending on the lake, coming straight toward them in a moving cloud. Descending on Alex...

She jolted upright in the chair, her heart practically beating its way out of her chest. It took a moment for her to realize she had dozed off in the hospital waiting room.

The steady hum came from the air-conditioning unit pumping cool air into the room. At the moment, the only threat to her safety was the vending machine full of cream-filled snack cakes.

Kate closed her eyes and tried to concentrate on her breathing.

That only managed to piece together a disturbing, all-too-real image of Alex's face when he *couldn't*.

A shudder ripped through her. Kate would never forget watching his color change to gray, seeing his eyes close.

She'd been so angry with him. And angry with herself, for falling in love with an exasperating man who thought he knew what was best for everyone but had no idea what was best for himself.

But years of talking to God—and listening

to His answer—had brought her around. She claimed that God didn't make mistakes. She knew He was never taken by surprise.

Kate had no idea how to move forward but she knew that God was right there with her.

"Kate?"

Her head jerked up at the sound of a familiar voice. She vaulted out of the chair and flew into the circle of Abby's arms.

Chapter Twenty-Two

❧

"How is he?"

"Stable." Kate choked out the word.

"We caught an earlier flight after Matt called." Abby managed a watery smile. "Now I know why they call it the red eye."

"They kept him overnight for observation, but the nurse said he should be able to go home late this afternoon."

Home to Chicago, now that Abby and Quinn were back.

Kate shook the thought away. It was where Alex belonged. Where he *wanted* to be.

"I had no idea that Alex was allergic to bees," Abby murmured. "He got stung a few times when we were kids, but other than a little swelling, he was fine."

"The doctor said it can happen like that sometimes." Kate suppressed a shudder. "I don't think Alex would have made it to the hospital if Grace hadn't found us when she did."

Kate had already dialed 911, but the nearest hospital was twenty minutes away and it would take the volunteer rescue squad at least that amount of time to arrive.

She was on the phone with the dispatcher when Grace, drawn to the cabin by the children's screams, had burst through the trees and found Kate bent over an unconscious Alex.

The social worker had taken one look at him and pulled a small cylinder from her bag.

"Grace carries an EpiPen with her because her nephew is extremely allergic to bee stings," Kate told them. "It prevented Alex's airway from closing completely until the ambulance arrived."

"Praise God," Abby said, tears welling up in her eyes.

Quinn zeroed in on the ridge of welts on Kate's arm. "How are you?"

"The nurse insisted on giving me a shot of

Benadryl to reduce the swelling." And calm her jangling nerves.

"Logan and Tori?"

"They spent the night at the inn with Grace and their aunt. Grace is bringing them to the hospital after breakfast. They need to see for themselves that Alex is okay."

"I'll bet he gave them quite a scare."

All Kate could do was nod.

In her mind, like a video that played the same footage over and over, she could see Alex running toward the lake, Tori clasped against his broad chest as a delegation of bees followed in aggressive pursuit. But then he'd stumbled and released his grip on the little girl. Gave her a gentle shove in Kate's direction before he'd collapsed.

"I want to see him," Abby said, her smile tremulous.

Quinn took her hand and together they walked out of the waiting room.

Kate stayed put.

Abby glanced back, a question in her eyes.

"Aren't you coming with us, Kate?"

"I'll stay here. I don't want to miss Grace."

It was thin as far as excuses went, but Kate wasn't ready to face Alex at the moment.

Or was it her feelings she wasn't ready to face?

Kate wasn't sure.

All she knew was that when Alex had stopped breathing, so had she.

The anger, the disappointment, it all disappeared. It no longer mattered if she lost the café or her apartment.

What mattered was that Alex was all right.

"I colored a picture for you." Tori clambered up on the bed and handed Alex a piece of paper.

He tried not to wince when the sheet scraped across his skin.

"I'm...blue." With red polka dots.

"Uh-huh." Tori nodded solemnly.

Logan sidled up to the side of the bed. One eye was swollen shut and his bottom lip puffed out, but the majority of the bee stings had landed on his hands as he'd attempted to protect his sister.

"You have polka dots, too, bud."

The boy's expression didn't change. "Are you...okay?"

"I will be when I can eat a cheeseburger instead of green Jell-O."

That comment earned a tentative smile.

"You have another visitor, Mr. Porter." Alice, the nurse who'd been peddling the lime Jell-O, poked her head in the room.

Alex's heart flipped over.

Kate?

He knew she was still in the hospital. Abby had told him that she was waiting for Tori and Logan to arrive, but here they were, accompanied by Grace Eversea.

Alex had been a bit taken aback when he'd met the woman. Kate had mentioned that she and the social worker were friends; but, for some reason, Alex had pictured an older woman, world-weary and as pale as the fluorescent light bulb in her cubicle. Not someone in her mid-to-late twenties whose laughing, espresso-brown eyes matched the leather cowboy boots on her feet.

"There he is!" Mayor Dodd marched in and came to a halt at his bed side. "You look terrible, Mr. Porter. Stopped by the Grapevine and picked up a few of Kate's cinnamon rolls. They'll cure what ails you."

"Thanks." Alex forced a smile.

The reminder of what he'd done to Kate hurt more than the welts covering his body. More than his throat, scratched and tender from the tube the E.R. doctor had inserted into his airway.

The fact Kate hadn't come to see him was proof that she hadn't forgiven him.

Alex didn't blame her. He hadn't forgiven himself.

"I have to make a phone call, Mr. Porter." Grace backed toward the door. "Tori? Logan? We can come back in a few minutes."

"They can stay here."

"Are you sure?"

Alex nodded and handed Logan the remote control. "Anything but the nature channel."

The siblings wedged themselves into the vinyl chair by the window while the mayor opened the box of cinnamon rolls.

"Something smells good."

Alex saw Matt Wilde framed in the doorway, Zoey at his side.

"Help yourself," the mayor said. "There's more where this came from."

Alex didn't have to wait long to find out what he meant.

As the morning wore on, people began to stream into his room like ants at a picnic—to see him.

Delia Peake and Liz Decker. Jake Sutton, Emma and Jeremy.

The Davis brothers and a few other teens from Kate's youth group.

Even Grady stopped by.

Alex could barely look the old cook in the eye. He could only assume that Grady hadn't heard the news yet. But right before the man left, he leaned down and looked Alex straight in the eye.

"You'll make it right."

He knew.

Alex's throat had tightened then, only this time it had nothing to do with a swarm of angry bees.

He wished he had the confidence Grady did.

By the time lunch rolled around, Alex's pillows had been fluffed and thumped and he'd been patted, cooed at and smiled upon more than one of the newborns on the maternity floor.

People who had been strangers two weeks ago waltzed into his room, bearing gifts of food and bouquets of flowers, as if they'd known him for years.

He'd never felt so vulnerable.

So…humbled.

"A little overwhelming, isn't it?" Matt, the only one brave enough to ignore Nurse Alice's not-so-subtle hint that Alex needed to sleep, smiled as he pulled a chair closer to the bed. "But you'll get used to it. You're part of the family."

"Family?"

"When you accept what Jesus did for you on the cross, you're born into God's family. You're one of His children."

Matt made it sound so easy.

"I don't deserve this. Any of it."

"None of us do. That's why it's called grace."

"I gave Mr. Porter something to help him sleep." The nurse, Alice, put a finger to her lips as Kate approached. "He kept muttering something about 'only a few more hours.' I assume that means he's anxious to leave. Some men are like that. Terrible patients because they hate feeling out of control."

"I won't stay long. I just want to…see him."

"You and everyone else," Alice muttered. Her eyes twinkled. "Not that I blame you. That man is quite easy on the eyes!"

Easy on the eyes, not so easy on the heart, Kate thought as she slipped into the hospital room. The curtains were drawn but she could see the outline of Alex's form in the narrow bed.

Gingerly, she perched on the edge of the chair and leaned forward to study him.

Raised, scarlet bumps disfigured the angular jaw. The sable-tipped lashes fanned out in the hollow shadows below his eyes.

He was still the most handsome man Kate had ever seen.

Unable to stop herself, she curled her fingers around his. Squeezed her eyes shut to staunch the tears that threatened to spill over.

"Kate."

Her head jerked up. She hadn't wanted to

talk to Alex—only see for herself that he was all right.

"I didn't mean to wake you up." She rose awkwardly to her feet.

"Didn't." Alex blinked up at her, looking strangely vulnerable in the blue hospital gown.

"How are you feeling?" Kate's hand itched to smooth a swatch of hair off his forehead.

He gave her a lopsided smile. "Only slightly better than I look."

"The nurse said you'll be released in a few hours. I should let you get some rest." Kate would have moved away from the bed but Alex caught her hand.

He frowned when he saw the welts on her arm.

"You got stung."

"Only a few times." Kate had stopped counting at seven. She tried to tug her hand away but Alex held her fast. "Not as many as you."

"Abby always said I have to be first at everything."

How could Alex joke about it? When Kate closed her eye she could still see that cloud of bees. Hear the children's cries for help.

"I should leave." Kate's thumb drew a circle on the back of his hand before she released it.

"What time is it?"

"Three o'clock."

Alex struggled to sit up. "Why are you here?" he rasped. "You only had twenty-four hours."

Twenty-four hours to come up with the money to buy the café.

Was that what Alex had been talking about when the nurse mentioned that he'd seemed agitated?

Tears stung Kate's eyes as she gently pressed him back down. "Stay put or I've have to call Nurse Alice."

The sheets hissed as Alex shifted restlessly beneath them. "You went to the bank, though."

He saw the answer in her eyes.

"Kate." He groaned her name as if he were in pain. "Why not?"

Because she'd followed the ambulance to the hospital and she'd been there ever since.

"It wouldn't have mattered. They wouldn't have given me a loan. Not for that amount."

Kate tucked the blanket around him. "Do you need anything before I leave?"

"Yes. I need you to forgive me."

Even though Kate didn't move, Alex felt her retreat.

She'd let the café go.

No, she'd *lost* it. Because of him.

Alex's throat began to swell again, but this time he couldn't blame it on the bees.

"I'm sorry. For everything." The words sounded so empty but Kate accepted them with a nod simply because that's the kind of woman she was.

"I forgive you," she said quietly. "It wasn't your fault that Jeff made the decision to sell."

A space of only three feet separated them and yet it felt like a chasm.

With a flash of insight, Alex realized that it wasn't Jeff's decision to sell the café that had damaged their budding relationship, it was *him*. Believing he knew what was best for her.

I changed the family motto. Don't settle for anything but God's best.

Alex wanted to find out what that was, even

if it meant stripping everything in his life down to its foundation and building something new.

Something better.

"Kate, I have to tell you—"

"*Don't*. Please." Kate scraped up a smile. "I don't want you to apologize. Or try to fix anything."

She knew him too well. But Kate had been right when she'd claimed that he didn't know her at all.

"What you did for Tori and Logan...thank you," she said softly. "And I'm glad—I'm glad you're all right."

Kate walked toward the door and Alex couldn't do anything—say anything—to stop her.

Regret sliced through him.

She might have offered her forgiveness, but Alex wasn't sure she would ever trust him with her heart.

Chapter Twenty-Three

From her rooftop garden, Kate watched the sunlight shimmer on the water, teased by a light breeze.

Her guests were running late today, so she'd taken advantage of the moment to curl up on the chaise longe and soak in a few moments of quiet.

Lucy and Ethel were draped over her feet, happy to have her home.

Kate wasn't sure how long she would be able to call it that. When the café sold, there was a good chance she would lose her apartment, too.

She'd spoken with Jeff Gaines's secretary and the woman politely informed her that

Jeff was out of the area on business but she should carry on "as usual" until he returned.

Easier said than done; but Kate was trying.

She had convinced Jenna Gardner to spend a few days at the inn while she became reacquainted with her niece and nephew. She'd hung out with the girls from her youth group. Looked at the photos of Europe that Abby and Quinn had taken on their honeymoon.

The only thing Kate hadn't done was say goodbye to Alex before he'd left for Chicago.

Abby had told her that he'd packed up and left within hours of being released from the hospital.

What had she expected?

They not only lived in different states, they might as well live in different galaxies.

This was real life, not one of the romantic comedies the girls in her youth group loved to watch.

Alex wasn't going to ride in a white horse and tell her that he loved her...even though she'd fallen irrevocably in love with him.

And just because Kate had spent an hour the night before surfing the internet for pictures of the Porter hotels—Porter Lakeside was her favorite—didn't mean she would ever leave Mirror Lake.

Not that Alex had asked her to.

Unfortunately, accepting the truth didn't make Kate miss him any less. She missed his smile like she missed green grass in the winter. She missed seeing him every day. She missed arguing with him…

Downstairs, she heard the door of her apartment open and close.

"I'm up here, Mr. Lundy!"

The breeze sifted through the stack of napkins, lifted them up and sent them cartwheeling off the table. With a squeak, Kate tried to chase them down before they reached the wall and fell like confetti onto Main Street.

"Gotcha!" Kate dived for the last one and held it up, a triumphant smile on her face. "If only Coach Dickens could see me now. I'll bet she would have let me run the fifty-yard dash instead of filling up water bottles…"

"I'll bet she would have, too."

The world suddenly tilted on its side.

Alex stood at the top of the stairwell.

Say something, Kate. You were talking in complete sentences when you were one year old!

"I—I thought you were in Chicago."

"I was. But now I'm back."

"Why?" The word slipped out before she could stop it.

"It's Sunday, right?"

"Yes." Kate watched Alex warily as he padded toward her, his gaze intent on her face.

"I'm here for dinner. It smells good, by the way."

"Irish stew," Kate murmured. "But no one else is here yet."

Why wasn't anyone else here yet!

"I know." Alex stopped a few feet away from her but the traitorous breeze carried the scent of his cologne right to her nose, which somehow sent a message to her knees to start shaking. "I asked them to wait awhile."

"You asked them—" Kate licked her lips. "Why would you do that?" And even more disturbing, why had her friends listened to him?

"I wanted to talk to you. Alone."

The words hung in the air between them.

Alex pulled an envelope out of his pocket and handed it to her.

"What's this?"

"You'll have to open it and find out."

Kate unfolded several sheets of paper and found herself staring at what looked like the deed to the café.

"This is in my name."

"It belongs to you now. Jeff and I came to an agreement."

"I don't know what to say."

"I could tell you, but I made a promise to myself I wasn't going to do that anymore."

Kate almost smiled.

"I can't accept it, Alex. It's too much. If this is some sort of apology—"

"It's not."

"But—"

"We can talk about it after you open this." Alex handed her a small box wrapped in tissue paper.

Kate's fingers tangled in the colorful topknot of curling ribbon. "Should I open it now?"

Alex nodded. It almost looked as if he were...nervous. Very un-Alex-like.

Kate slid into a chair at the bistro table and peeled off the wrapping. Wading through several more layers of tissue paper, she unearthed a porcelain trinket box. A bee skep, complete with one of the tiny winged assassins perched on a delicate lavender blossom.

"You mentioned that sometimes you bought one of these to match with a memory."

Kate swallowed, reliving those horrible moments when Alex had collapsed on the ground.

"You want me to remember the day you almost died?"

"No, I want you to remember this one."

Alex knelt down beside her and opened the lid.

A diamond solitaire winked up at her. Now it was Kate's turn to stop breathing.

"I love you, Kate, and I want to spend the rest of my life with you. Right here, in Mirror Lake."

Kate didn't answer. Couldn't answer.

"You want to *live* in Mirror Lake?" Kate could hardly comprehend it.

"It grows on a person."

"You'd be giving up everything."

"I'd be gaining everything. 'What good is it for a man to gain the world yet lose his very self,'" Alex quoted softly.

"Everything I want is here. I want Mr. Lundy to beat me at chess every Sunday. I want to help Jeremy and Cody finish that tree fort before winter. I want to make sure Tori and Logan are all right.

"I want to sit on the porch and watch every sunset with you." He touched her cheek. "And every sunrise."

Kate slid off the chair and backpedaled away from him.

Alex's initial panic subsided a little when he saw the diamond ring still cradled in her hand. She hadn't thrown it at him—or over the side of the roof. He figured that was a good sign.

"You almost died," she stammered. "You aren't thinking clearly. People say that kind of thing can change a person."

"I'm sure it can, but the change happened *before* that. I had a long talk with Matt that day…and then a long talk with God. He'd been trying to get my attention for two weeks. Post-It notes and sand castles and potluck dinners.

"If that crazy bee attack taught me anything, it's that God is in control, not me. We don't know how many days we have on this earth, but I know I want to spend them with you."

Kate sniffled and Alex tilted his head toward the sky.

"Can you believe this? I'm getting all mushy and she still hasn't said yes."

A ghost of a smile touched Kate's lips. And then just as quickly, it disappeared.

"What about your hotels? Everything you worked so hard for. You can't just walk away."

"I don't expect you to move to Chicago but I'd like to keep Porter Lakeside. It's the first hotel my parents owned and I think you'd like it. Very charming and old-fashioned. Tony and Jessica even said you can mess around in their kitchen when you visit. The rest…I'll sell. Abby already gave me her blessing."

"What if you get…bored?"

"Not gonna happen," Alex said instantly. "Mayor Dodd already signed me up to help with Reflection Days and we're going to be busy with the house."

"What house?"

"The one we're going to build. The one with the really nice kitchen," Alex added because this was taking a lot longer than he thought it would and he wanted to kiss her again.

Kate looked away. "I didn't mean you'd get bored with the town. I meant…you might get bored with *me*. I'm not beautiful and sophisticated and worldly and, well…look at my watch!" She held up her wrist.

Alex bit back a laugh when he realized Kate was serious.

"You are beautiful," he said softly, advancing on her. "And I don't want sophisticated and worldly, Kate. I want you."

"We argue all the time."

"Think about how much fun we'll have making up."

Kate's cheeks turned fiery red but she didn't protest when he slipped his arms around her waist.

"I don't want you to change your life, Kate. All I'm asking is that you make room in it for me."

Kate closed her eyes, certain that when she opened them again she would be lying on the chaise longe with a sunburned nose and a houseful of people who were wondering why she was taking a nap when she was supposed to be making dinner.

It was a dream, she didn't want to wake up. And if it wasn't…

She opened her eyes a crack. Alex was looking down at her.

Waiting.

She took Alex's hand and carefully set the ring in his palm.

The look of pain—and disappointment— that flashed in his eyes arrowed straight through her.

"Is there anything I can say to make you change your mind?" he said tightly.

"No." Kate put out her left hand. "Because I love you, too."

When Alex realized that she was accepting the ring, not giving it back, he groaned.

"What you do to me, Kate."

Kate flashed an impish smile. "What do I do to you, Mr. Porter?"

"You make me want to be one of the good guys." Alex slipped the ring on her finger and drew her into his arms again.

You already are, Kate wanted to say. But she decided to wait until after he kissed her...

"Did she say yes, yet?" A voice floated up the stairwell.

"'Cause we're hungry!"

Kate gasped.

"Who's down there?" she whispered.

"Everyone," Alex whispered back. "If you said no, they were going to help me convince you."

Kate clucked her tongue in mock disapproval. "I thought you promised to change your ways. You obviously had this all planned out."

"No, but I'm pretty sure God did."

"I'm pretty sure He did, too," Kate said softly.

"Something we agree on," Alex teased. "It's a start."

Kate stepped into the shelter of his arms

and right before his lips claimed hers, she smiled.

Yes.

It was a *very* good start.

* * * * *

Dear Reader,

I couldn't wait for Kate to get her own happy ending—or should I say beginning! I knew it would take a special man to win her heart, and I kept going back to Alex Porter, Abby's older brother who barged on to the scene in *A Place to Call Home*. Just as I suspected, he and Kate were meant to be together!

Many times when I'm working on a book, I find that I'm learning lessons in faith and life just the way my characters are. Jesus's parable of the wise and foolish builders reminds me that there is no other foundation able to withstand all the storms of life.

Some of you may know that the writing of this book was delayed while I underwent radiation treatments for breast cancer last summer. The prayers and letters of encouragement I received from readers like you were such a blessing. I am happy to report that I am back to normal (well, as normal as a fiction writer can be, I suppose!).

I hope you are already looking forward to your next visit to Mirror Lake, when popular columnist Jenna Gardner arrives to care for her niece and nephew. This city girl is totally out of her element—until wildlife photographer Dev McGuire steps in to help. Watch for a special cameo appearance by one of the McBride sisters *(Family Treasures),* too!

Please stop by my website at: kathrynspringer.com to say hello and sign up to receive my free newsletter. Not only is it a great way to connect, you will know when to plan your next trip to Mirror Lake!

Keep smiling and seeking Him,

Kathryn Springer

Questions for Discussion

1. Describe your hometown or city. What are some of the things that make it unique?

2. Do you think that Kate and Alex are examples of "opposites attract" or do you think sparks fly between them because they are so much alike? Explain your answer.

3. How did Alex and Kate's childhood experiences shape the decisions they made as adults? If you had to pinpoint a "defining moment" in each of their lives, what would it be?

4. Why did Alex think that Kate was "settling" by staying in Mirror Lake? Have you ever had someone disagree with a major decision you've made (a move, career change, etc.)? What was your response?

5. When does Kate begin to change her opinion of Alex? Have you ever had to

change your initial impression of a person once you got to know them better? Describe the situation.

6. Kate loves to bake. What are some of the things you enjoy doing? Do you prefer to spend time alone or with a group of people?

7. Alex teases Kate about being a superhero because she does so much. Just for fun, if YOU were a superhero, what kind of "superpower" would you like to have (ability to fly, become invisible, etc.)?

8. What was the turning point in Alex and Kate's relationship?

9. Matt reads the parable about the wise and foolish builders. What are some of the "foundations" people build their lives on?

10. Kate has a special collection of trinket boxes that she "matches to memories." Do you have a collection of some kind? What is it?

11. Knowing how busy Kate was, her friends surprised her with a potluck dinner. Has anyone ever done something like that for you? What was it?

12. Alex didn't realize that he had a "grand plan" until Kate brought it to his attention. Having a plan can be a good thing, but it can sometimes get in the way of what God has planned for us. Have you ever found this to be true in your own life?

13. How did Alex's proposal signify the changes in him? Do you think Kate changed, as well? Give examples to support your answer.

14. Imagine you are Alex and Kate's wedding planner! What would their wedding be like?